LUKE CHRISTODOULOU

MURDER ON DISPLAY

VINCI
BOOKS

Vinci Books

vinci-books.com

Published by Vinci Books Ltd in 2026

1

A CIP catalogue record for this book is available from the British Library.

Paperback ISBN: 9781036713614

The EU GPSR authorised representative is Logos Europe, 9 rue Nicolas Poussion, 17000 La Rochelle, France contact@logoseurope.eu

By Luke Christodoulou

Greek Island Mysteries

The Olympus Killer
The Church Murders
Death of a Bride
Murder on Display
Hotel Murder
Twelve Months of Murder

Dedicated to my son, Iasona (Jason).
Welcome to this world!

Chapter One

Midnight arrived on the exotic island of Folegandros, a small island shaped like a tilting eight; falling into the clear pure waters of the Aegean. Away from the town center and the tanned-from-the-Greek-sun tourists, lay silent, dark neighborhoods. The locals had long gone to sleep.

A blue wooden door stood slightly ajar and warm light from inside crept out into the darkness and the cool summer breeze that roamed through the snakelike roads of Chora. Whispering words of love and the exchange of passionate kisses broke the silence.

'Shh, I've got to go. My mother has been calling me for the last hour. You know how she can get. If I don't get home soon, she will send out a search party,' eighteen-year old Natalie said softly, her auburn hair gently caressing her bare shoulders.

'Stay, my love. How many opportunities do you think we are going to get? My wife will be back on Thursday,' her older lover complained, holding on to her hand.

'I can't,' she replied, failing at hiding her annoyance.

Nothing irritated her more than a man that begged. She pulled her slender hand out of his strong hold.

'Good night,' she said and forced a smile. He was a good lover after all.

She dashed down the paved street, along picturesque, classic Cyclades homes. All were painted blue and white, some out of choice, some forced by the local council in the name of beauty and attracting tourists. Dim light fought to escape its glass lamp post prison and reach the rock-laid road. Natalie called her mother, apologizing for not answering her cell phone and in her tender, sweet voice -the fake voice that she used often- informed her mother that she was on her way home. She looked down on her phone's screen as she ended the call, unaware of the shadowy figure approaching from outside her periphery.

A faint scream escaped her red lipstick mouth when she raised her head and came face to face with the boy limping towards her.

'For fuck's sake! You scared the shit out of me.'

'You... You... should... not swear, Natalie. It is not... nice for a lady... to talk like that,' he replied, in his slow manner of speaking, well-known in his small town. He struggled with breathing, pausing nearly after every other word.

'Really, retard? You're giving me advice?'

Just by uttering the word, she felt bad. Her consciousness kicked in after she saw the sorrow spreading across his baby blue eyes. 'Sorry,' she rushed to add and maneuvered to pass her wobbling, chubby former classmate.

Adonis stepped in front of her. 'Why the hurry?' Pause. 'Stay, talk with me.' Another pause, longer this time. Cold sweat formed across his wide forehead, below his blond hair that blew around carelessly in the windy dark alley. 'You talk to all the boys,' he added, struggling with his hectic breathing.

Remorse quickly died inside her. 'What's *that* supposed to mean?' she asked, raising her voice. 'Besides, I only talk to the good-looking boys. Have you seen yourself in the mirror, freak?'

Natalie pushed past him and quickened her pace.

Just a few miles away, her mother, Electra, sat in her hand-made rocking chair by the large kitchen window that overlooked the precipice of Chora. Her greyish hair was tied up high in a bun, shining in the moonlight that got lost in the deep wrinkles across her face. At only fifty-nine, Electra looked at least a decade older. A farm girl, raised in the fields, worked for years under the cruel midday sun, bore and lost six children during her thirties before finally giving birth to twins at the not-so-youthful age of forty-one. Her joy was short-lived as her husband died of a heart-attack two years later. Forced back to work as a cleaning lady at Chora Resort and Spa and raising two kids on her own, time had not been kind to her tired body.

With slightly trembling hands, Electra raised her hot Greek coffee to her chapped lips. Knowing her children were on their way home, she smiled as the hot beverage travelled down, offering comforting bliss to her strained body.

'How you manage to drink hot coffee in this heat, amazes me,' Gregory's husky voice made her jump.

'And what would have me drinking, my son? A frappe? A freddo cappuccino? Or maybe a mojito?'

Gregory's laughter warmed her better than the strong steamy coffee.

'How's working at the bar for the summer coming along?' she asked, patting the worn-in armchair beside her.

Her lanky son approached, kissed her tenderly on her fore-head and settled next to her.

'Money's good...'

'Money isn't everything...' his mother interrupted him. 'You should be having fun on your last summer before Uni.'

'I am, mama. The music's great, I drink for free, my mates all come round and I meet girls. What more can a guy ask for?' he replied with a mischievous smile gracing his handsome face.

'I hope local girls and not those slattern, easy European girls on holiday.'

Gregory placed his hand upon his mother's. He raised his eyebrows and looked into her beady eyes; the portal to her fiery soul. 'Now, that's just bordering racist.'

'I don't care what it is. I care only for you and your sister.'

'Where is Natalie, by the way?' Gregory asked, before his mother got too *worked-up*; his favorite word to describe her passionate speeches about her children.

'She called, said she was on her way home. She was at Melina's.'

'I bet she was,' Gregory muttered and sprang up. Thankfully, his mother's ears did not catch his words. She was drowsy after a long day of cleaning and serving.

'What's that, boy?'

'I said, good night. I'm off to bed.'

'Good night, my treasure.'

Soon, both had drifted away to dream land. Gregory in his single bed, under the posters of pretty girls on big bikes and first league football teams, dreamt of life in the big city. Fall was approaching quickly. Electra dozed-off in her rocking chair, staying there to hear her daughter return to the family nest. Yet, hours later, sun rays attacked through the window, spreading light around the minimal kitchen and Natalie had not yet returned home.

The bright Greek sun slowly rose from the Aegean Sea and began illuminating the narrow streets. Old-lady Persephone, a woman of ample proportions, was first to open her blue wooden door, releasing the tantalizing aroma of freshly-baked bread. Her black-clothed figure ambled across her long yard and picked up the garden hose by the gate that had grown golden with the sunrise. Her flower-filled garden offered her much pride and Persephone struggled hard to maintain her flowers during summer's scorching heat waves. Her trick was to water them early in the morning before the flaming sun dried up the earth. As the perfumed scent of her red roses surrounded her, she looked around.

Her fragile throat grappled to voice her strident screams. The green garden hose fell from her shaking hands and Persephone stumbled backwards before falling to the wet grass. At eighty-two, and after witnessing a World War as a child, eras of depression, eras of oppression, the violence in the world from her television, her husband's body after his fatal car crash, Persephone had thought nothing could shock her anymore.

She thought wrong.

The sight on the rooftop of the abandoned house opposite her garden brought her to her knees. A mutilated, headless, nude body had been speared through the house's cut, rusty antenna pole. The woman's breasts had both been sliced off, leaving behind two round bloody patches. Her stomach had been sliced open and her insides were dangling out, dripping blood upon the grubby roof tiles. Persephone closed her eyes, prayed for strength and placed her hands on the moist ground, pushing herself up. As

5

much as her elderly body allowed, she rushed towards her house. Screams from the town square echoed around and followed her into her home, letting her know she would not be the only one calling the police.

Soon, people had gathered by the closed coffee shops and tavernas of the 'middle' town square -the town boasted three in total- and, sighting the brutal crime, stood motionless in complete shock. Never before, had a murder taken place on their tranquil island. Even the island's lone police officer had frozen below the gruesome display. At the youthful age of twenty-six, Valentina had only two years of service under her gun-carrying belt. In those two years, she had dealt with a couple of bar fights, a case of domestic abuse and a few cases of stolen wallets. Mostly, she kept the one-room police station clean and presentable, and brewed coffee, which she enjoyed while checking her Facebook page. Totally unprepared, she sealed off the area around the deteriorating, dilapidated cottage and called the mainland headquarters.

Chapter Two

CITY OF ATHENS

Ioli pulled off her silver hair tie and unleashed her silky black hair. She rubbed her lower back using considerable force as she leaned forward in her milky-colored, office chair that lately housed a special, expensive cushion ideal for pregnant women. She lifted her head up slowly and exhaled deeply. Staring down at her enormous -according to her- baby bump, a smile grew across her face. She could not believe how quickly six months had flown by. She still could not believe she was pregnant. Quite often, she would end up feeling guilty when caught up at work, she would forget that she was carrying. Now, there was no forgetting. She moved slowly, had to use the police headquarter elevator to reach her office on the third floor and lost her breath more often than her grandmother lost her glasses.

She glanced through the glass wall in front of her desk and observed her useless -again, according to her- rookie of a partner, Alexandro. A rather short, humorous, handsome guy with too many muscles to count, a desire to help and please, and a permanent grin across his youthful face,

Alexandro had quickly become Homicide's new favorite addition. He spent most of his coffee breaks outside, enjoying his Greek, Assos cigarettes, discussing football, politics and women with comrade smokers from the police force.

Ioli sighed as she witnessed him delivering coffees to fellow homicide detectives while retelling the same joke as he went. She twirled her chair around and her eyes saddened at the sight of my empty desk behind her. Her former partner, mentor and best friend, I had been on leave for the last year.

'Fucking pancreatic cancer,' she whispered and reached for her cell phone. Her fingers scrolled down to 'C' and she pressed the call button.

'Hey, boss,' she said as soon as the call connected.

'Please tell me you need my help on a case. Tracy has been off work since yesterday and she is driving me mad,' my rough voice boomed through the receiver.

'Shut up, grumpy. Your wife is perfect and you know it!'

'She is trying to persuade me to go on a cruise. Me! On a ship, imprisoned and forced to relax.'

Ioli could not help, but laugh. 'You do realize you sound ridiculous, right?' She paused and found the strength to ask. 'Can you go? I mean, with chemo and all...'

'That's the thing. I have finished with this round of therapies and my doctor wants to stop me for a while...'

'Stop you?' Ioli interrupted, fear coloring her trembling voice.

Now, it was my turn to laugh. I threw my hairless head back and let out my uproarious laugh. 'My God, your mind always goes to the worst scenario. I'm fine. She just wants to take a step back to see what the chemo has managed. I'll tell you more when we meet. Now, concentrate on my nightmare. Because I have a month free of chemo, Tracy took time off work and wants us to go on a cruise across the Aegean. Your job is to talk her out of it!'

'I will do no such thing. If my girlfriend thinks it will do you good, I'm behind her.'

'Women,' I grunted.

Ioli stood up and watched as Alexandro, *the rookie*, followed two senior police captains into the chief's corner office.

'Costa, I got to go. My kisses to Tracy,' she said quickly and hung up the phone. With her deep set eyes focused on the group of men entering the scariest place of homicide HQ, Ioli approached the glass door of her office. It was only when her hand grabbed hold of the aluminium handle that she realized how sweaty her palms were. Ioli never did sweat. She guessed she could add this to a long list of changes going on with her body. Ignoring fellow co-workers' stares, she dashed down the long hall and rushed to the only wooden door on the floor. The chief was old-fashioned in all areas of his life and his office door had survived through various renovations for the last fifteen years or so. The chief's deep bass, croaky voice carried outside. It helped that Ioli's ear lingered only inches from the door. The random clear words did not form a sentence in her head. Bravely, she knocked and entered without waiting to hear the chief's signature yelling of 'come in'; always shouted, always colored with tones of annoyance. The chilly conditioner-produced air attacked her sweaty pores. Of the chief's long list of things that irritated him, the heat would easily crack the top five.

The three men stood towering over the chief's long mahogany desk. The greyish-haired, nearly sixty-five-years-old, burly chief sat in his custom-made, pitch black office chair with his back toward the impressive view of the bustling metropolis of Athens. The fierce Greek sun illuminated the glass towers that dominated the horizon and light bounced around the spacious office.

'... so it's one of you two that needs to go...' the chief was saying, as she invaded the normally off-limits-if-not-invited office of the man-in-charge. His military background was salient in the way he ran things.

The eyes of the two captains widened and Ioli could swear that even their shaven, broad jaws lowered. Only Alexandro smiled at her; his innocent, goofy grin coming to life across his unlined face.

'Sorry, boss,' she rushed to say. 'I did not realize you had company. I have the report on the Petraki case...'

'No, you saw your partner being pulled in here with two captains and realized I was about to team him up with one of them because you are pregnant.'

Ioli could not resist smiling. Beaming, she replied 'Rookie is off my hands?'

'No, he is still your new partner. There has been a murder on Folegandros and I am sending either Andrea or Gianni to accompany Alexandro...'

'Wait. A murder on an island is my case. Captain Papacosta and I are in charge of any homicides on the islands...'

Now, their jaws definitely dropped. Rumors circled that once, back in the nineties, someone had interrupted the chief, but it was more of an urban legend around the department.

'Well, you're carrying and Costa is on medical leave till further notice. I am not sending a six-month pregnant girl to Folegandros in this freaking July heat wave. Besides, everything indicates this to be an open-and-shut case. The local authorities have already arrested the murderer. I am just sending a team to help with evidence and processing so nothing goes wrong in court. It will be a good experience for Alexandro and it would do him well to pick up some pointers from a veteran captain.'

Ioli stood silently for a moment, apparently processing everything she had just heard. 'According to the constitution of our department and the categorization of homicide cases according to geographical location, all murder cases from the islands are mine and Costa's jurisdiction. This case belongs to me and I am not on maternity leave, yet. I have a substitute partner and we will take the case. As you said, it's an open-and-shut case. No need to waste precious veteran time. I am sure there are more complicated cases for these experienced captains to lead. As you said, it is just evidence collection. Besides, the fresh sea air would do wonders for my baby boy.'

She felt like panting, yet fought it and managed to remain cool. Her eyes stayed locked on those of the chief's as she witnessed his expression softening. As much as the expression of his steel face could.

'It's a boy?' he remarked and a toothless, semi-smile appeared. 'Wonderful. Now, Cara, come on. Wouldn't you rather relax? You are entitled to leave.'

'I'd rather do myself and Costa justice in continuing our job.'

The chief raised his hands up and exhaled deeply. He swung his chair around and gazed out the wide window. Without turning back round, he calmly asked the two captains to leave. 'Take the case file, Cara. Everything you need to know is in there. Get Mary to call and set up the police ferry. Get to Folegandros, ASAP. I don't need island amateurs ruining evidence and filling up tons of useless forms and testimonials.'

Ioli's smile broadened upon her face, raising her high cheekbones. She picked up the brown envelope from the thick wooden desk and before the chief had any time to regret his decision, she hastily exited the cold room.

Alexandros turned to follow.

'And kid?' the chief's deep voice stopped him on the spot.

'Yes, sir?'

'Take care of her or it will be the last case you'll ever see. The filing department is always in need of a new pair of hands.'

Chapter Three

Valentina's green eyes stayed focused on the florescent light on the aging air-conditioning unit hanging from the 'begging for a fresh hand of paint' blue wall, opposite her untidy, worn-in desk. She stared at it for a good whole minute; she gazed in disbelief at the low temperature the screen promised. Inside, the lone police department of Folegandros felt like Dante's lowest level of Hell. Maybe, the menacing heat wave was not to blame. Maybe, it was her nerves. She had made her first arrest just hours ago. Her eyes moved across the room and travelled to the single holding room. Adonis had cried and sobbed since she locked him up. Now, total silence. She figured that the teen had finally fallen asleep for siesta. Valentina never got much sleep. She usually slept on top of the department's filthy bunk bed and tossed and turned while dreaming of escaping the small island. Looking across at the time on her computer screen, she thought of the morning she had had. The tremendous sight of the headless body on display, the moment the villagers recognized the victim to be one of their own by the girl's arm tattoo, and the taunting scene that replayed inside her mind; Natalie's mother Electra running to the town square. Electra had dropped to her knees and screamed uncontrollably; animal-like sounds came out of her as she kicked and cursed, curled up on the ground. Even her son froze and did not dare approach her. Thinking back, the girl's brother remained rather cool, Valentina thought. She stood up and approached her prized possession; her silver, high-speed frappe maker. She threw two full spoons of coffee into the turquoise plastic cup and roughly the same amount of sugar. It was going to be a long day. Police officers and the coroner were coming from the mainland. She wanted to prove herself sufficient and professional. Maybe get promoted and transferred to another station, one with a bigger task force. Loneliness was her permanent roommate; Valentina spent eight-hour shifts inside of the station all alone. Just her and the creepy fat spiders that lived in the corners, high above her head. At least, they ate invading mosquitoes and stayed up there, in their well-crafted webs.

She unlocked the top drawer of her desk and looked down at the bloody knife; the large, sharp-bladed knife with the obsidian handle and the name ADONIS carved into it. She had found the murder weapon next to the crumbling wall of the abandoned house that had had the disgraceful honor of displaying the dead body. She had found it as she manically wrapped the police yellow tape around the building.

She threw a couple of perfectly-shaped ice cubes in her sweet-smelling cup, prayed for strength and sipped the much-needed beverage. Euphoria journeyed through her. 'Greeks and their passion for coffee,' her Dutch ex-boyfriend used to say whenever witnessing her ritual of making and devouring coffee. She remembered Andriaan fondly. His tall, muscular build, his thick, carefree blond hair, his heavenly laughter... her place on his long list of lovers. For her, he was her first real love; for him she was just another summer fling. It took her two Adele albums and a significant amount of vodka to get over the fact.

Valentina sat back down in her cheap office chair, gathered her platinum blond hair to her right shoulder and let her mind drift back to morning memories. Comedy and tragedy; both born in Greece, both always living side by side. She had walked up to Adonis's two-story house where he lived only with his grandmother. Quite comically, under the circumstances, the entire village followed her. Valentina stood outside the blue wooden chipped door, one hand on her firearm, the other ready to knock. The door flew open before she reached it and startled her. If not for such a tragic crime, she was sure the crowd behind her would have laughed.

The cries of his grandmother and the begging on her knees would remain forever engraved in her memory. The seventy-two-year old lady with the white hair and the burgundy apron, yelled at her that she was making a terrible mistake. 'My boy is innocent. My sweet child could not have done such a horrific crime. Adoni, tell them,' she screamed and shrieked. Tears flowed down her furrowed, thin face; her fists clenched tightly as she hit the floor and begged the Holy Mary to help her. Adonis, on the other hand, remained expressionless, lost in his confused mind. Valentina wondered if the boy even knew or comprehended what was going on.

'You are being arrested, Adoni,' she had said into the boy's ear, yet received no reply. Adoni did not utter a single word as he passed among his fellow islanders that watched in shock; some even in disgust. No one spoke. Angry crowd mentality was imminent and Valentina hurried to take the youth into custody, safely away from the people gathering outside. Only behind closed doors did Adonis break down and cry. He sobbed all morning until Morpheus offered him the sweet escape of sleep.

As Valentina contemplated earlier events, the police ferry bounced upon the ever-moving, dark blue Aegean Sea and undulating waves crashed perpetually into the high-speed boat.

'I wanted to become a coroner, I said. Thought it would be perfect for a lazy ass like me. And, oh, the peace and quiet. No patients of mine would ever complain,' Jacob Peta, the jovial, rotund coroner chatted away, while consuming a feta and bacon sandwich. 'Nowhere cooler than a morgue, I thought,' his rant continued. 'But no, I had to become a police medical examiner and get dragged around from island to island under the scorching sun!'

'How can you eat on the boat?' Alexandro asked, his eyes drowsy and heavy, his mouth hardly opening out of fear of losing this morning's breakfast of a *berries and egg* smoothie. Alexandro sat curled up on a green wooden bench that was screwed to the ferry's wall, just outside the ship's small bridge. He watched and listened to the coroner, fascinated by his bubbly personality.

Jacob stopped his monologue and his Greek pacing up and down, and turned in Alexandro's direction. He bit down on his third breakfast for the day and laughed. 'When you sign your life away and finally get married, kid, and your wife makes you go on a diet of rabbit food, you will have your answer.' He, then spun back around to look at newlywed Ioli, hoping to catch a glimpse of her trademark *Julia Robert* smile. Ever since I -her partner and his good friend- left the force due to my cancer treatment, he had not heard her laugh like she used to.

Ioli had her back towards them. Her head lay upon her arms that were stretched out on the metal railing. She gazed down on the rhythmic percussion of the short-lived waves and her eyes followed them running up to die upon the sandy shore. Her eyes strayed only when the ferry approached Karavostasi, Folegandro's only port, and the mountainous island came into sight. The 20-meter vessel slowed down as it entered the turquoise hued waters of the natural bay and its dozens of fishing boats seemingly flying as the waters were utterly clear; enabling you to see every fish, crab and rock from above. The long concrete pier ran into the sea, the only thing steady in the picturesque scene; it played like a high-definition movie before Ioli's eyes. Ioli stood up, her right hand firmly on the railing, the other on her growing tummy. The ferry bumped against the car tires that hung along the cold grey side of the dock and came to a stand-still. Alexandro hopped off from the side and exhaled in relief as his feet hit solid ground. Jacob chuckled at the young man as he ripped open a bag of shrimp-flavored chips.

'My dietician does allow sea-food,' he joked, witnessing Ioli's rather disapproving look. He carefully climbed down the boat's hot-from-the-sun, aluminium steps and having reached his concrete destination, turned and extended his hand to Ioli.

'I'm pregnant, not disabled,' she said, as she lowered herself down with ease.

'And, then you modern women grumble about *where have all the good men gone?*!'

Ioli finally smiled and tenderly placed her hand upon his shoulder. 'I see our ride is here,' she said, her eyes travelling down the lengthy pier all the way to the young officer with the shiny boots, the well-ironed uniform and the Ray Ban shades.

Ioli walked ahead as the two men followed. Alexandro enjoying the serenity and the beauty of the surroundings and Jacob enjoying the last crumbs of Elysium taste that lay on his fingertips.

Ioli introduced herself and extended her hand, while trying not to get annoyed by the officer's not-so-subtle stare at her belly. Alexandro rushed to introduce himself with a wide smile as he had just noticed the ideal-for-a-short-guy blonde with the curvy figure. Jacob waved from afar and approached the parked vehicle.

Jacob squeezed his overweight body into the front seat of the dusty Mazda 3 with the brand-new police stickers on its side. Valentina opened the back door for Ioli, waited for Alexandro to sit next to her and then jumped into the driver's seat. With the turning of the key, the engine came to life and the party of four were on their way to the crime scene. The car passed small, white-washed houses, many of which had been converted to tavernas, souvenir shops and kiosks. The tourist wave that swept the neighboring islands of Santorini, Naxos and Paros, had gradually reached the shores of Folegandros. The vehicle also passed by the indiscreet stares of locals who had heard of the terrible crime that was committed in their central town. Ioli gazed out at grandmothers doing the sign of the cross, first on their bodies, then towards the car, blessing them.

'Jesus's fan club is strong here on the islands,' Jacob quipped and chuckled at his own jest.

'If I was Jesus, I would spend most of my time on the Greek islands. No where prettier,' Alexandro commented and secretly searched for a reaction from Valentina. A slight smile was all he needed.

Soon, the village of eighty inhabitants was left behind; a miniature town in the rear-view mirror. Fields of lonely olive trees and overgrown weeds surrounded them on both sides; fields that ran all the way up to the blue-water horizon that embraced them.

Ioli felt her cell phone vibrations in her jean's right pocket. It was a message from Mark, her husband. Just then, did she began to concentrate on the on-going conversation in the car. The two men were discussing tomorrow's big football game with Valentina. Ioli never understood girls who liked football. She had long classified football as a sport tailored to satisfy men's premature and brutal nature. She always smiled as she watched Mark curse the TV, uttering profanities she would only use if she burnt dinner or if she found her favorite restaurant closed. Food was the only sport she found worth worrying about. Ioli replied to Mark, apologizing for not texting -as she had promised- that she had arrived well. Then, she rolled her eyes at the juvenile remarks made about each other's team and interrupted them.

'Do you have your case file with you, officer?'

'Yes, ma'am,' Valentina replied, switching from her friendly tone to a more professional one, and leaned over to Jacob's side, opening the glove compartment. She lifted out a big, brown envelope. Not that such a size was needed; she had only taken three pictures and her notes resided on a single piece of plain A4 paper.

'Give the pictures of the body to the coroner and pass me all your notes.'

'Damn,' the coroner said, and waved the first photo to the back of the car. Ioli studied the photo that reinforced her opinion of humans being the true monsters in this world.

'Poor girl. No one deserves to die like that. I guess it must be a shock for your small community. Was she well-liked around the island?' Alexandro asked.

'You could say that,' Valentina replied, her eyes focused straight ahead.

Ioli glanced out from her notes, looking for a facial expression on the young policewoman with the enigmatic answer.

'These are just notes of what happened. Where are your statements?' Ioli asked.

'Statements?'

'You did ask around to find witnesses, right?'

Valentina's face began a journey from Greek-white skin to rosy cheeks. 'Well, I found the murder weapon and...'

'You didn't ask around?'

'Well, I spoke with her brother and he said she was at her best friend's house. I have called the friend in, later today, so you can speak with her and that way we will have a timeline.' She exhaled quietly. 'I am by myself here, I couldn't leave the station and Adonis alone with a vexed mob outside. I taped off the scene and covered the body...'

Seeing the beaming look on her face as she stated her *accomplishments*, Ioli could tell that she was supposed to be pleased.

'The body is still there?' Jacob asked, his eyes opening wide.

'Where would I take her? And who would I get to help me get her down? It would contaminate the scene. I thought, it would be best for you to collect evidence.'

Ioli said no more. A single thought ran freely through her brain. It was going to be a long day.

'Did you dust for fingerprints?' Alexandro asked.

'Of course! Now, listen here. I know my job. I might not have much experience, but I do know how to collect finger-prints. I scanned both the fingerprints of Adonis and the ones of the murder weapon and emailed them to the lab in Athens. Results should be back by now.'

Alexandro gently smiled. 'I did not intend to insult you. I am, also, new to homicide cases.'

The next five minutes of the fifteen minute route were made in silence. All you could hear were happy crickets singing in unison, scattered across the centuries-old olive trees.

Ioli, having visited the majority of the Greek isles, was not easily impressed by views and beaches. But the town of Chora left her in awe.

White boxes with blue doors and railings gathered into a group and filled the hilltop all the way to the edge of the 200-meter cliff. Snakelike, rock-paved roads ran amongst them, yet it was the winding dirt road journeying uphill out of the postcard-perfect town and leading to the impressive church of the Holy Mary that caught Ioli's eye. An aura of freedom surrounded the entire landscape. All against a background of a turquoise sky and the deep blue sea. Ioli rolled down her car window. She had guessed right. The air was pure, clean and carried the freshness of the sea along with it.

There were no grassy areas to be seen. The strong winds and the lack of rain allowed only the most stubborn olive trees and bright green-leaved lemon trees to grow. In the town, the scenery switched to a plethora of flowers and deciduous shrubs. Flower pots were dotted along the pave-ments and hung from houses' walls.

Valentina parked rather abruptly in what seemed like the middle of the road.

'This is the furthest cars are allowed,' she justified herself, and signalled them to follow her.

Ioli got out of the vehicle and stretched her arms up high. Her lower back reminded her of the life growing inside her. Multiple banners and posters were tied to the stone wall opposite her. Elections for mayors were next week and campaigns were at their peak. All politics in Greece were heated conversations and over-the-top campaigns. For a country that gave birth to Democracy, there were a hell of a lot people wishing to rule over others.

Jacob, also, lifted himself out of the car with difficulty. He exited with his nose sniffing the air like a hound dog on barbeque day. The aroma of freshly-watered roses and lilies embedded itself on his nasal hairs. 'I miss the pollution of Athens, already,' he chuckled.

They followed Valentina down a wide path that led to the town's square.

'Town square... whoever killed the girl wanted people to see her. Has the boy you arrested talked? This seems like a revenge crime. Some sort of punishment. To humiliate her in the eyes of the town,' Ioli spoke, mostly thinking out loud.

'Hasn't said a word. He just cries. Whenever I speak to him, he just stares at the floor and rocks back and forth. Don't know if you read it in the file, but he isn't very bright. He is... *special*, you know?' Valentina said, before declaring 'here we are'.

The abandoned house stood out from the rest. It stood in the line of houses opposite the rows of chairs from the multiple coffee shops and tavernas that circled the square. Its white paint had faded, revealing the mud brick wall beneath. Its wood and hay roof sagged terribly. Gaping holes showed where windows had once been, while its subservient-to-the-elements door hung on its rusty hinges at a jaunty angle.

All three newcomers stood shock-still at the sight of the bagged body impaled on the antenna pole. Valentina had her back to the scene, signalling to the town folks whispering from the tavernas to remain where they were and to stay quiet. Nothing harder than keeping Greek island village folk from uttering their opinions and asking an array of personal questions to the 'outsiders'.

Ioli's eyes finally left the bagged body and circled the scene. The 'sealed un-professionally with too much police tape' scene. 'The Tasmanian devil would have taped this scene better,' she joked softly into Jacob's ear.

'How do we get up there?' Jacob asked, swallowing his laughter. Valentina stood feet away.

'Just like the killer. There are stone steps around the back leading to the roof,' Valentina replied. 'Be careful, though. Stay in the center of the steps,' she added, her eyes weighing the heavy coroner and his over-stuffed backpack. Valentina could not help but wonder what he carried around in it. Ioli's small, black, leather briefcase was easier to judge. Gloves, camera, evidence bags, fingerprint kit, plastic bottles, special flashlights and powders probably all neatly in place.

Jacob caught her eyes focused on his rucksack. 'I swear, not even half of it is food,' Jacob joked and Ioli chuckled.

'It's his tent. We will cover the roof. Too many alert and prowling eyes,' Ioli said, and turned the corner.

She placed her case on the first step and unclipped its hinges. She took out her camera and began snapping away. A trail of blood drops revealed that the murder did not take place on the roof. Soon, the rest of the group joined her and warily went up the disintegrating stairs.

'He wanted her to be found. To be seen...' Ioli spoke softly as she took photos of the area. 'Is he capable of such logic?' she turned and asked the island's officer. Valentina shrugged her shoulders. 'Maybe we could ask his former teachers? I don't know if there is a doctor that he might have visited on another island. We don't have one living permanently on the island'.

'Maybe there is no logic. Maybe something he copied from a movie or a book?' Alexandro spoke from behind her.

'That's a lot of maybes. Maybe he has a dark place in his fragile mind,' Ioli commented.

'Don't we all?' Jacob asked, and with heavy puffing, stepped onto the roof.

On the roof, Valentina's eyes ping-ponged from Jacob to Ioli as in a matter of seconds they unfolded the thin, silky-looking sheet with the four hooks at its corners and clipped it to the sides of the roof, passing over the body, quickly creating a pavilion covering the entire rooftop.

Ioli exhaled and ran her fingers across her forehead.

'You okay?' Jacob asked.

'Fine. A bit hot.'

'When are you due?'

'Mid October.'

'I'm a Libra, too,' Alexandro said, his crooked grin spreading across his beaming face.

'Great,' Ioli said, trying to hold back her natural sarcasm. 'Will you do us the honors, Mr. Jacob?'

Jacob approached the antenna with the pool of still liquidy blood below it and unzipped the body bag all the way to the top. He, then pulled the bag off entirely, revealing the maimed naked body.

Alexandro whistled awkwardly. 'I'll be honest; I've never seen a body so viciously attacked. Headless with guts hanging out like that. Poor girl.'

'A mutilated doll played with too roughly,' Jacob Petsa said, observing the body's exterior.

His eyes ran up and down her body, ignoring the already present putrid smell and the black flies -donkey flies as his grandma used to call them- buzzing around her disembowelled stomach.

'Such a dehumanizing murder...' Alexandro said.

'Guess you haven't seen many dead or abused children,' Jacob commented drily. 'Now, girl, what's your story?' he asked what was left of Natalie's body. 'You know...' he redirected his voice in Alexandro's direction. '...a body was made for living. When it dies, it always yearns to inform how it ceased to live.'

Ioli tilted her head, squinted her eyes and circled the body.

'Maybe you and Valentina should go find where the trail of blood began. Take some shots of where the murder weapon was found. Then, go talk around the square. Someone must have seen or heard something in such a quiet place.'

'On it, Cara,' Alexandro said and off he went; his stomach heaving, not yet settled from the swaying sea.

Jacob wore his white gloves and took the girl's hand into his. Natalie's icy fingers were forever trapped into a defensive fist. 'I see no wounds and her nails appear clean. She did not see this coming. She must have clenched her fists when she was first stabbed.'

'There are two entry wounds in her back,' Ioli commented, taking a pair of tweezers and taking samples of the mud and grit that surrounded the wounds.

Jacob focused on the raw pink flesh where the girl's breasts once were. 'I'm guessing these were made post-mortem.'

'What about the decapitation?'

'Also, post mortem. Why cut off the head if the girl's dragon tattoo makes it clear who she is?'

'Perhaps our killer took it as a trophy. A souvenir of the murder. Maybe to shock.'

Ioli, now, stood behind him, looking at the thick scarlet rivers running down the girl's thighs. 'Was she stabbed between the legs?'

'Looks that way.'

'Maybe, she was raped?'

'I need to get the body back to Athens and perform a proper autopsy to get a clear picture,' Jacob said, breathlessly standing up. 'Working in this heat is as exciting as tepid coffee.'

'I'll get Alexandro back up here to help you with the body and Valentina will drive you back to the ferry. We'll be in touch.'

'Ioli?' His voice put a stop to her fast pace.

She turned around. 'Yes?'

'How's Costa?'

'Under the circumstances, he is fine. He has stopped chemotherapy and guess what? As we speak, Tracy has dragged his ass on a cruise across a dozen islands or so.'

Jacob's heavy chuckle escorted her down the bloody steps. She held her belly and controlled her breathing. Her mind wandered to what I was up to at that precise moment.

Chapter Four

July; the busiest month of the year at Piraeus port. Ships, both cruise and cargo, covered the majority of the deep blue waters of the man-made bay. It was only ten o'clock in the morning, yet you could still see the asphalt desperately trying to breath. I always loved that. The waves above the road, distorting the image received by our eyes. I guess the natural phenomenon excited me as it served as proof that nothing is as it seems. Never trust your eyes alone.

'Costa, what the hell are you thinking about again?' my lovely-after-her-morning-coffee wife, Tracy, asked as we stood in queue to board the newly-renovated Neptune II.

'Nothing, dear. Just thinking of all the fun we are going to have. Drinking cocktails and making love like teenagers...'

'Bull,' she said and giggled. 'You have that silly look upon your face. I know you are thinking of something strange. Like why are certain leaves greener than others or how come shrimp are the cockroaches of the sea or how are the waves above the road created by the heat or...'

'You are starting to scare me, woman. Get out of my head.'

Tracy leaned in closer to me and placed her head and her now short, bright red hair on my chest. 'Never,' she said and looked up into my eyes. We kissed and as we pulled away from each other, we realized that we were holding up the line.

The group of twenty or so teenagers behind us giggled and chuckled at the sight of the two still in-love fifty year olds. This is the point where Tracy would want me to clarify that she was still just forty-nine. Fifty scared her. It was the number she considered as the point where surely you had more yesterdays than tomorrows.

Their teacher coughed loudly and on purpose, her eyes running from side-to-side, behind her black-framed reading glasses. The students silenced at once and a pretty, blonde girl whispered in broken English 'sorry, Mrs. Anne.'

'Must be an expensive private school. Taking the kids on a ten-day cruise around the isles,' Tracy said softly, as we picked up our luggage and moved closer to the ticket-checking booth.

'They don't all look Greek. Maybe an international school...' I started to say before being interrupted by a bored-looking, unhealthily skinny woman with a white shirt and a red tight skirt. 'Tickets, please.'

'Why didn't you name the ship Poseidon?' I asked as Tracy took care of everything procedural.

'Excuse me?' the lady asked, her tired eyes struggling to look up to mine, located at six feet four.

'Neptune is the Latin name of the God of sea. It's a Greek ship sailing the Greek islands. It should be called Poseidon.'

'There's a complaint box on board, sir. Here you go, ma'am. Have a nice journey. Next!'

'Maybe I should ask for better and friendlier staff,' I replied as Tracy pulled me by my oil-green shirt.

'Can't take you anywhere,' she laughed and rolled her eyes, as we crossed the narrow temporary bridge, following behind the spotty-face youth that took our luggage.

I looked back and said goodbye to solid ground. With a guilty smile, I saw the lady at check-in exhale in dismay at the pile of tickets and ID cards placed in front of her by Mrs. Anne Jackson, the head-teacher of the travelling group of eighteen-year-olds.

After a three-minute walk through a maze of corridors and similar doors with different numbers, the young boy came to a halt outside cabin 202. He unlocked the door, placed our suitcases down and extended his right hand. 'Everything comes at a price, hey kid?' I joyfully said and shook his hand. It was only when he felt the five Euro note in his fingers that he smiled. A short-lived smile as he rushed to leave, to go back out and earn more needed-for-college tips.

'Isn't it lovely?' Tracy said in pure excitement as we entered our upper-deck, two-room cabin.

I looked around at the new wooden furniture, the carpeted floors, the glass door that led out to a miniature balcony and the hanging gold-plated chandelier. Through the open doorway, I saw the king-size bed with red sheets and the box of chocolates laid upon them.

'How much did *this* cost?' I spurted out as my heart skipped a beat.

'Always a helpless romantic!'

'Oh, come on. You know what I mean.'

Tracy approached me and placed her arms around me.

The weight I had lost due to chemotherapy aided her arms to meet behind my back. Her perfume surrounded me and lured me closer. 'It's my present to you. For being you. Big, strong, still-alive you. Now, shut up, enjoy the cruise and make love to me.'

With every passionate kiss, an item of our clothing fell to the floor. Our naked bodies were soon, side by side on the soft mattress. So familiar, so in-touch. Sex in your fifties can still be amazing. Even better than in your horny teens and your energetic twenties and thirties. Don't let anyone convince you otherwise.

It was great to feel the warmth of being inside Tracy, once again. My sex drive had taken a bungee jump and never came back up during chemotherapy sessions. Nothing worse than for a man to mentally crave sex and then witness his body not following; not up for the task.

Lost in each other's familiar embrace we felt the ship move and set sail for our first stop, the scenic island of Syros.

As my eyelids began their descent, booming music suddenly invaded through the thin cabin walls.

'I think we have the luck to be next to the senior high school kids,' Tracy mumbled and covered her head with the spare pillow. Tracy could sleep through a nuclear apocalypse. I, on the other hand, could stay awake from the buzzing of a pesky mosquito or the ticking from Tracy's silver wristwatch.

I stood up, located my black boxer shorts, put them on and exited to the balcony. An endless view of shimmering, blue waters sparkling in the presence of intense sunlight welcomed me. The air was fresh, clean and pure, sprinkled with that unique salty smell of the ocean.

'This planet is too beautiful. God, I don't want to die.' I gazed

up into the clear sky and let my eyes become watery by the searing sun. *'At least, not by cancer. Not now. I'm too old to die young'.*

Inside the cabin, Tracy's smile faded as she watched me get lost in deep thought. She was, also, in conversation with God. *'I buried a child, I do not wish to bury a husband. Let me go first.'*

Chapter Five

Ioli watched as the police car sped off in a hurry. She carefully took a few steps back as the swirling hazel blur of dust approached her.

'*Lovely islands, third world conditions,*' she thought, picturing the body lying on the back seat of the car behind Valentina and the coroner. The island had no hospital, thus no ambulance. Ioli, thought about the island having only one doctor and he did not even live on the island permanently. If Mark knew that his pregnant wife was on an island with no medical assistance, it would surely have been the beginning of an argument.

She turned to Alexandro, who stood beside her, waiting for her orders on how to proceed.

'Why do you have that grin permanently placed on your face?'

Inappropriate or not, it felt good to get the question that had nested in her mind out there.

Alexandro chortled awkwardly. 'My mama's friends

used to ask her that about me when I was a kid. She used to say it is because I'm happy.'

'What do you say?' Ioli asked, her eyes fixed on his.

'I guess I am. Maybe it's my shield against the evils in the world.'

Ioli studied him for a second before replying. 'Work on making it a smile then, rather than a grin.' And before the conversation on the subject could go on, she continued, 'go to the boy's house. Ask his grandma if you can search the premises even though you hold no warrant. Tell her it has been issued in Athens. It should be ready by now anyway. The girl's head has to be somewhere. Don't be intrusive. Be kind to the old lady and win her over. Talk about Folegandros, the weather and such, and then direct the conversation to Adonis. Friends, places he liked to hang out, what kind of kid was he and so on.'

Alexandros listened carefully to her every word. He wanted to prove himself worthy in Ioli's eyes. He did not reveal it, yet he was an ambitious young man. He had plans to climb the *police hierarchy ladder* and needed to add experiences and successes under his belt.

'On it, boss,' he said and marched off, down the dirty paved road.

Ioli could not fight back a flat-line smile. *On it, boss* echoed in her ears. That was her line for so many years. She never wanted to be someone's boss. She was fine with being part of a team. But some cells that took the path of abnormal growth and a cancerous tumour had changed all that.

Ioli decided she would enter her *friendly-mode* and mingle with the locals at the coffee shop opposite the crime scene. She resisted taking out her cherry-red note pad out of fear of scaring willing witnesses away and aimed for an affable conversation.

Greek islanders have inbuilt welcoming natures. The heavy shop owner with the heavier mustache rushed to fetch her a chair while his wife brought her over an ice-cold, homemade lemonade. Both asked about her pregnancy and if she required anything else. It wasn't easy squeezing inter-rogation questions among casual ones while avoiding answering anything about the crime to the group of locals that gradually surrounded her.

Her mind worked overtime *writing* down all the details she had acquired.

As she thanked everyone and strolled down the road, heading towards the police station, one fact stood out in her head. They all spoke kindly about Adonis, yet no one had anything nice to say about the victim. They spoke with apathy about Natalie, while smiles were born as they spoke about the eighteen-year-old boy that she was about to meet.

The narrow road between the smooth grey stones that served as sidewalks, unfolded before her eyes like an abstract painting. Colorful rocks formed the road; their clean colors revealing that cars were not allowed through, while the layer of dust settling upon them declared that they had not seen rain for months. The street curved and opened out like a sloppily discarded belt. Ioli slowed down to look at all the quaint houses with the well-maintained gardens and the blue wooden fences. Many hosted posters with smiling politicians, with bold-lettered sentences of promises they probably would not keep. Election season was in full swing. The view between the houses was breath-taking; a magical screensaver of endless blue. She, also less-ened her pace as her maternity trousers made her sweat uncomfortably under the scintillating sun. She gazed up at the menacing ball in the clear sky, its sunrays running down like molten lava, burning all in its destructive pass. The heat reminded her of the half-empty bag of Jelly Babies in her pocket. *'Poor babies are melting,'* she thought and pulled the bag out. To her relief, the colorful sugar-loaded babies were still intact. Ioli picked up her first two victims. Both red. She never blended her flavors. Just minutes later, as her eyes fell upon the humble building with the outdated POLICE STATION sign, Ioli ate the last piece of candy.

The 90's police car was parked badly outside. Valentina had returned from dropping Jacob 'The coroner' Petsa and the unlucky young woman for whom Ioli was responsible to serve justice to. 'Thank God, she's back,' Ioli said and exhaled deeply, trying to catch the breath that seemed to elude her often. The last thing she needed was to sit outside a locked door under the midday sun.

The shabby door mat welcomed Ioli's flat shoes -she surely missed her low heeled shoes that her gynaecologist no longer allowed- as she dusted them off before entering the cool room. Icy conditioned air settled on her hot skin, cooling every pore, offering much needed sanctuary from the high temperatures outside.

Valentina leapt out of her chair upon seeing her enter. A kind-faced, elderly lady sat opposite her wearing a pitch-black dress that fell to her tired ankles, a pearl necklace and a worried look. A nylon bag was placed on the floor by her right ankle.

'Ioli, this is Mrs. Sophia, Adonis's grandmother and legal guardian. She wishes to see him, but I said she had to wait for you.'

Ioli felt that Valentina spoke mostly to apologize to the woman who had been begging her since her return from the port. Mrs. Sophia had sat outside the station ever since the crowd dispersed after Adonis's arrest.

'Nice to meet you,' Ioli said and extended her hand. 'If you don't mind, I'd rather talk with you for a while and then see Adoni alone. After that, you can have all the time you wish with him.' Ioli's fake wide smile spread across her high cheek-boned face.

Mrs. Sophia's facial muscles remained still; unsure of how to respond. Her heartbeat elevated to heights even her pink prescription pills could not control. She lived only for her grandson. He was all she had. She lowered her watery eyes and exhaled.

'I understand, my girl. You have to follow, what do you call it? Protocol. Do things right?' she said, lifting her head up gradually and Ioli caught a glimpse of a trembling smile. 'I'll do my best to be patient. But, I tell you now. My boy is innocent. I swear this by all the Saints and the Mother of our Savior, Jesus Christ. Blessed be his name and all that call for him.'

Ioli sat down opposite the lady, studying her. She was your typical Greek grandmother. Olive oil skin, white hair, dressed in black -mourning the loss of a husband or a child, deep sun-produced wrinkles, worried eyes, a genuine smile and an aura of *proudness*. Ioli thought of her own grand-mother and how she should call her more often.

'You raised Adoni on your own?'

Mrs. Sophia smiled. 'Best thing I have ever done in my life. My daughter had him out of wedlock. She was studying in Sweden at the time. She never told the father.'

'And where is your daughter, now?'

Mrs. Sophia slightly licked her top lip, sighed and then, gently bit down on her bottom lip. 'You have kind eyes, my child. But, I see sorrow lurking behind them. You know how cruel and unjust this world can be.' Mrs. Sophia lowered her head, once again. 'Overdose. Adoni was only four at the time. My Helen never could cope with our reality. She needed her escapes,' she continued, then lowered her voice, 'I blame the drugs for Adonis's difficulties. But, God works in mysterious ways and maybe it was for Adonis's best that my unfit-for-a-mother daughter passed away. Adonis has special needs and her home was not the place for it. Here, with me, he has a good life, a happy life.'

'What exactly are Adonis's difficulties, as you said?'

'Body wise, he has a crooked knee joint that forces him to limp. Mentally, doctors said he would never grow older than a nine-year-old. He is an eternal child locked in an adult's body. He has such a gentle and innocent nature. He is not capable of such a gruesome crime. Even, if it was possible for him to kill, he hasn't got the brains to do what the killer did to that poor girl. Please, Lieutenant, you have to help us. You have to prove my boy is innocent.'

'So much for an open-and-shut case. Collecting evidence, my ass,' Ioli thought as she scribbled down Mrs. Sophia's statement. 'Where were Adonis's whereabouts last night?'

'He left home around nine o'clock. He finished his chores, watched his favorite movie, what's it called now, Wall-E. Yes, the one with the robot. Then, he went for a walk. It is a safe town and everyone knows him. He hangs around the coffee shops, playing tavli, and drinking lime and lemon. His favorite.'

Mrs. Sophia glowed as she talked about her grandson. *'Her love for him is intense. He is her everything'* Ioli wrote down, next to notes to have Alexandro check the boy's time line. Her mind quickly thought of her new partner and how he was going to find a locked house.

'And, what time did he get home?'

'Oh, dear. I am seventy-two years old. I was asleep by then. However, he was in his bed when I woke up at six and his clothes were beside his bed. Clean as a fiddle. I brought them with me. I know, now-a-days, you have all these modern gadgets and stuff. Analyze them, prove my boy innocent,' she said, her voice trembling more than usual. She picked up the nylon bag and extended her hand to Ioli. Ioli carefully took the bag without touching any of the items of clothing overflowing from it and placed it on the desk to her right.

'I will. Mrs. Sophia, I promise you that whomever is responsible for this crime will pay.'

'Thank you, my dear. May the Lord bless you and your child.'

'One last question. How do you explain the knife? I mean, the murder weapon is your grandson's, right?'

'Yes, it is,' she said, exhaling loudly. 'But, anyone could have taken it. Adoni is always leaving his things here or there.'

'Thank you Mrs. Sophia,' Ioli said standing up. 'You have been very helpful,' she said and offered a sincere smile. 'Now, I think it's time I met Adonis. Though, he is technically an adult. I'd rather see him on his own first. You two are close and I imagine seeing you right now will make both of you emotional. I need to get some answers out of him. If that's alright with you.' Ioli paused, waiting for a reply. The old lady's sky-blue eyes were fixed on her lips.

'I guess I could be a little more patient. I'll leave. That small room is no place to talk. Let him out. Talk with him here.'

'Thank you,' Ioli replied and shook the woman's hand. Ioli watched as she trudged to the door.

'I'm going to make Greek coffee,' Valentina said from

behind Ioli. She had been hovering around her since Ioli had sat down. 'Lieutenant Ioli? Coffee? Frappe?'

'Doctor advised me to cut down on my coffees. Anything cold,' Ioli answered as the old lady closed the door behind her.

'Got my mama's home-made lemonade. Lemons from my grandpa's...'

'Excellent,' Ioli interrupted her and made her way to the lone cell in the building. 'Make one for the boy, too.'

As Ioli placed her hand on the cool, metallic door handle a loud beep echoed through the high-ceiling room with the heavy, thick, wooden beams. Valentina had noticed the tiny red light flickering on the station's phone. She pressed the button to listen to the message received.

'Message received at ten A.M. and twelve minutes,' the robotic voice came through the round speaker.

'We were at the crime scene,' Valentina commented before silencing to listen to the incoming message.

'Err... Hi, Valentina this is Sakis from the shoe repair shop. Err... I was hoping to speak to you in person, called a few times before. This is not something I feel comfortable discussing over the phone. Please come around to my shop. Adonis is innocent. I know who killed Natalie...'

The prolonged, high-pitched *beep* signalled the end of the words that left the two officers with their eyes wide-open.

'Call him back, get him to come in and give a statement. If he fears being seen here as it seems; he did mention you going around to his shop, make an appointment, to be there in half an hour. I'll get Adonis's statement and we can go meet him,' Ioli said and Valentina nodded in reply.

Ioli opened the holding-room door and stood to the side. No one appeared. She waited a few seconds and cautiously ducked her head into the scanty-for-a-cell, magnolia-painted room.

Adonis sat curled up at the edge of the bottom bunk bed. His head rested in his crossed arms that lay upon his trembling knees. Yet, his eyes peeped through and he studied the tall woman opposite him. She seemed beautiful. She seemed nice. She had a great figure. The type of woman his nana always said was trouble. The type of woman his mother used to be. Before the drugs. Before the endless array of criminal boyfriends.

'Adonis?'

'That's my name,' he thought and raised his head.

Ioli smiled kindly and focused on his blue eyes. 'Adoni, I am Lieutenant Ioli Cara. Come out, let's have a nice, cold lemonade.'

Adoni giggled uncontrollably; his frantic breathing getting in the way. Pretty girls never asked him to join them for a drink.

'Relax,' Ioli said and winked at him. With a tilt of her head, she invited him to follow her. Valentina had already placed two ice-cold lemonades on the small round table that had three legs.

She, also smiled at Adonis before turning to Ioli. 'Mr. Sakis is not answering. Probably closed the shop for siesta.'

'Do you know where he lives?'

Valentina nodded that she did. Ioli could not make up her mind if the young girl was too lazy to reply verbally or if this is how young people communicated nowadays.

'Okay, give me ten minutes and we will be off.' She turned her attention to the shy boy whose eyes eagled in on the lemonade. 'Sit, have a drink.'

With a smile as wide as the canyon of Vikos, the young man-boy picked up the refreshing beverage with the orange straw and sank back into the tall-backed office chair. As Adonis slurped down his cold drink, Ioli pulled her chair closer and sat down.

'You have a baby in your belly. A blessing. Be a good mama.'

'Yes, I have. And I will do my best to be a good mama.'

'Do more than your best.' Adonis's tone deepened and his lemonade-caused smile flatlined a second. 'Did my nana sit here?' he continued with his usual joyful tone. 'I can... smell her perfume.'

'Yes, she passed by and...'

'Can... Can I see her?' he asked, his puppy-like eyes opening wide. 'Sorry, for inter... inter... interrupting you.'

'It's alright. As for your grandmother, she will come by later and visit you.'

His eyes lowered and the glass of lemonade trembled in his shaking hands. 'Can't I go home with her?'

'Not right now, no. Adoni, do you know what happened to Natalie last night?'

The boy nodded; the longest of his blond hairs falling in streaks to his eyebrows.

'Did you see her, last night?' Ioli asked, her voice steady and friendly.

Another nod. 'Where? What did you talk about?' Ioli aimed for an open-type question to avoid another nod.

'The alley behind the square... She was in a rush...'

A long pause followed. Ioli leaned forward and placed her hand on the boy's swinging knee. Her eyes inviting him to continue.

'I... I said hello... We talked... I wanted to talk more... Natalie is such a pretty girl, but she had to go home to her mama.'

'Adoni, do you know what time it was that you saw Natalie?'

Adonis shook his head.

'Was she alone? Did you see anyone else in the alley?'

He shook his head again.

Ioli sat back into her chair. 'A pretty girl, huh? Did you like her?'

'Very much,' he replied with his cheeks rosying up and a shy smile growing across his round face.

'Didn't she have a boyfriend?'

Adonis giggled. 'Natalie always had a boyfriend. But, sometimes she…she had more than one... I thought maybe I could be one of her many boyfriends.'

Ioli started to realize why none of the locals from the square had anything nice to say. Small island communities frowned upon such behaviors. Especially from girls.

'Who was her boyfriend at the moment?'

Adonis rocked back and forth before leaning forward; nearly falling off the edge of the chair. 'That's a secret,' he whispered.

'A secret? And do *you* know the answer?'

'Maybe.' Adonis began to laugh, and fell back into the chair.

'What's so funny?' Ioli asked with a wide smile, seemingly going along with his joke.

'All the boys... wanted her more now. Jake was upset she broke up with him... Sent her flowers every day... Andreas, too... He chased her everywhere, but... she always said no to him. Too ugly for Natalie.'

Ioli noted every word he said. 'Are these classmates of yours?'

'Yes. Only one senior class here. We all... grad... duated last month. Together.'

Ioli's hand fell softly upon Adonis's. 'And the name of the mystery man? The secret? I am good at keeping secrets, too. Part of the job.'

Adonis shook his head abruptly. 'Uh-uh. I swore by Saint George. I would never say his name. Nana says it's blasphemy.'

'Does Nana know who the man is?'

'No. No way!' The shock coloring his voice became strong and obvious. 'I would never talk... about things like this... with Nana!'

'What if I bring an icon of Saint George and you ask him if it is okay by him to tell me the name?' Ioli asked, hoping to get the name from the God-fearing boy.

'You're funny. No, no and no... No way. It is not right to break promises... promises to saints are sacred.'

Ioli sat up straight, disappointed. 'And how do you know who he is?'

'I saw them together.'

'When did you see them together? Natalie and...?'

'A couple of weeks ago.'

'Did they see you?'

Adonis nodded. 'Natalie ran after me and made me swear. She gave me a kiss in return.' His face lit up and he giggled while staring at the floor.

'I see,' Ioli remarked, then nodded to Valentina, who sat silently on the edge of her desk observing and recording the conversation. Valentina came forth, placing the *sealed off in a plastic bag* murder weapon on the wooden, three-legged table by their side.

Adonis shivered at the sight of blood and turned away in disgust.

'Is this your knife?'

'Yes,' he admitted.

'When did you last see it?'

The boy lifted his shoulders. 'I... I don't know. Maybe last week. I don't remember when I lost it.'

'But, you did lose it?'

He replied with a nod.

Ioli studied the boy. 'So, you did not kill Natalie?'

Adonis sat up straight. 'Me? No, no ma'am. Never. I could not even hurt a fly. Ask around... and you will see!'

'Not even a fly, huh? You know that's a line from a movie.'

Again, he nodded. 'Scariest movie I have ever seen. Nana doesn't know. Saw it at a friend's house.'

'He said he would never hurt a fly, but he was the killer.'

'Yes, but with me... it's true,' he replied with a grin.

Ioli sat up straight. 'Thank you, Adoni. That'll be all, for now. Miss Valentina will escort you back to your room...'

Adonis started rocking back and forth in the chair, sending leathery creaks throughout the low-ceilinged room.

'... just for a while. We have to go somewhere at the moment, but on our way back we will bring your nana with us, too,' Ioli said, thinking of how she promised to let his grandmother see him.

The word nana brought peace to the room and Adonis's heart. Reluctantly, like a stubborn teen forced to do one chore or another, he dragged his legs into the small holding room and fell face down on the hanging-from-the-moldy-wall bed. Valentina locked the door behind him.

'Off to the shoemaker?'

'At once,' Ioli replied. 'I want to get to the bottom of this. Hopefully, our witness will put an end to this sticky situation.'

'Sticky?'

'No way a court of law would jail that kid. We need to find the real suspect here.'

Valentina nodded in agreement and followed Ioli out of the building. Adonis's grandmother was nowhere to be seen. 'Well, at least we don't have to listen to her begging to see him,' Valentina said, locking the main entrance door with her noisy key ring. It was overflowing with keys and keyrings of flags and monuments Valentina dreamt to visit one day. They all rattled together as she locked the front door and continued their cacophony as she beeped open her car and started the engine. Not noticing Ioli's judgmental raising of her eyebrows, Valentina turned on the car radio and glad she found her latest favorite hit playing, she set off for Mr. Sakis' shoe repair shop.

Ioli buckled her seat belt, placing it across her chest and behind her back. She wanted no pressure on her tummy. The pressure on her brain cells was enough. *'Who listens to this crap?'* she thought.

Once again, Ioli found herself lost in the view and the smell of the Aegean blended with the flowery scent that travelled around upon the summer zephyr. As the car turned right and journeyed downhill, the postcard background disappeared and the pleasant scents faded, being replaced by an strong earthly one. The tires of the vehicle said goodbye to asphalt and headed down a well-flattened dirt track, raising clouds of dust into the air. Ioli studied Valentina, who drove staring straight ahead, never gazing into the sea, never enjoying the surroundings. Ioli was not one for small talk and she felt no urge to get to know the young blonde that wore too much make-up. However, she found herself asking Valentina, her favorite question for colleagues.

'So, how come a cop? Out of all jobs, why did you choose to become a police officer?'

The main reason she loved asking the question was because it was never the money, the hours or various benefits like you heard about other occupations. It was always because there was a cop in the family that inspired his children or a good story. Ioli loved listening to both. In Valentina's case it was neither; she was an exception to Ioli's rule.

Valentina was caught slightly off-guard as her inner-voice sang along to the radio. She lowered the volume and turned to meet Ioli's eyes, just for a split second, before returning to the road ahead.

'To be honest, I wanted a job that would get me off this island.'

Ioli's eyebrows journeyed upwards. Now, she knew why the girl never enjoyed the view. Disappointed in Valentina's reply, she pulled out her cell and was going to text Mark. She never did as Valentina continued, 'it's a wonderful place and I love my home, but it is just too small, you know? I thought if I became a teacher or a cop it would be my chance to see Greece. Get stationed somewhere new every few years might sound horrible to some, but for a poor girl like me it sounded like a golden opportunity. My luck! I get stationed here. I'm still pretty sure my mama called the chief and somehow sorted things out. Anyway, next year, hopefully I will get transferred.'

'Here we are,' she declared after a small pause, leaving Ioli no time to react to her answer.

The dust around the car quickly settled and Ioli found herself staring at a row of tall, tangled olive trees. A sign hung on one of them. SAKIS SHOE REPAIRS AND SALES. Through the gaps in the trees' branches, Ioli saw what was nothing more than a fixed-up shed, standing in the middle of a lawn belonging to an old cottage. A woman in her mid-fifties stood by the open house door, her right hand above her eyes in an effort to block out the bright sunlight.

'Hello there, Mrs. Julia, is Sakis in the shop?' Valentina called over to her as she stepped outside.

'Is that you Valentina? Oh my, you have grown. How's your mother? Say hi. Well, well that police uniform suits you well. Bravo, my dear,' the chatty lady replied. 'Sakis? He left twenty minutes ago to head up to town. Someone called him and he left in a hurry.'

'Who called him?'

The woman raised her shoulders. 'No idea. Was he expecting you? Silly man, going off when he knew you were coming.'

'Did he tell you we were coming?' Ioli asked, coming forward.

Julia studied her for a second. 'Yes, but he did not say why. He looked upset, yet I could not get a word out of him. He never tells me anything ever since my heart attack two years back.'

She walked closer towards them with every word.

Ioli gazed up to the scorching sun. She could not catch a break.

Valentina noticed the desperation growing on the pregnant lady's sweating face. She placed her hand on Ioli's shoulder. 'Has he got a cell phone with him?' she asked his wife, who without answering took out her own phone and called her husband.

'No answer,' she declared seconds later.

Chapter Six

ON BOARD

Tons of freshly painted steel cruised effortlessly upon the calm deep waters. The recent renovations that took place upon board were obvious. There were no signs of blisters in the paint, weather worn decks and rusty chains -signs of age met upon most ships condemned to sail under the Greek sun. Plain physics; nothing survives the heat untouched.

Tracy and I were walking back to our cabin, having enjoyed a dip in the east swimming pool of the ship. Like adolescents on a first date we journeyed together hand-in-hand, enjoying the fifty shades of blue that surrounded us. Tracy looked stunning in her turquoise bikini, a fit and toned forty-nine-year old. I, on the other hand, was your typical, middle age Greek guy with an overflowing beer-belly and thick hairs running across my legs and ganging up all over my chest and even my back. We both smelled of coconut sunscreen. I had placed a significant amount on my bald head. Used to having a healthy amount of black hair, I had never thought how much the sun could burn my scalp.

Soon, we turned into the interior of the ship, escaping

the ferocious sunrays and walking down the long corridor that led to the thin wooden door of our cabin.

As I closed the door behind me, I felt Tracy's warm hands pull down my green and orange trunks. She hugged me from behind as I stood there naked. Her hands ran down my chest, feeling my heartbeat accelerated and ventured downwards.

'The sea air suits you well,' I said, exhaling deeply.

'You being this relaxed suits me well,' she replied, letting go and cat walking to the bed. She laid down and invited me with her eyes, her body and her soul. Soon, I was in her, my arms wrapped tightly around her coconut-scented body; my lips travelling up her neck all the way to her ear lobe.

Suddenly, as I was biting her lower lip, a sharp smashing sound was heard from the adjacent cabin -like a large vase collapsing into a thousand pieces. A couple of thuds followed, then a drowned scream. We both turned our heads towards the direction of the magnolia-painted wall with the atrocious painting of a blunt bowl of fruit.

Silence.

Tracy read my expression.

'Silly kids,' she said, and raised her head out of her soft pillow. Her hot lips kissed mine. Mine remained still.

'Should I go check?'

'And get arrested for indecent exposure?' she joked.

'You think I am overreacting?'

'Teens trashing a room while on holiday is not an unheard of crime, Mr. Police Captain. I'm sure their teacher can handle this.'

I smiled and having noticed that I had started to go soft down below, I fell back down upon Tracy, my hands and lips moving around rapidly.

Later, happily tired, we drifted off to dreamland, safe in each other's embrace.

Frantic screaming woke us both. I turned my sore eyes towards the clock on the wall. We had been asleep for over an hour.

'That's not just kids being kids,' I said, jumped out of bed and rushed to dress. Tracy sat up, lost for words as more yells for help joined the girl's screeching.

As I exited the hallway, I noticed a group of six teens, all crying, all afraid to enter the room. Their teacher stood in front of them under the door's arch, her hand covering her trembling mouth.

'Oh, God,' she whispered.

A black boy, not older than nineteen, sat on the carpet-fitted floor behind them. Tears run freely down his youthful face as he leaned back against the wall. He kept on yelling: 'where's Holly? Where's Holly?'

I approached the teacher who looked up at me suspiciously.

'I am a police officer, ma'am. What seems to be the matter?' I asked calmly.

She took a step back and with her hand, she showed me the open door. She was in no condition to speak.

I have witnessed many crime scenes in my life, but never one with such a large pool of blood. The blood had yet to dry. The crime was fresh. Guilt came over me. It probably took place during mine and Tracy's love-making session. I knew I should have checked.

Such a large amount of blood, yet no body in sight.

The purple vase with the yellow thin lines was scattered across the floor below me. It must have been thrown to the door. The room was a mess with clothes and shoes covering the majority of the single beds and the two armchairs. A pink jewelry box laid by the sizeable puddle of life fluid. Both of its miniature drawers had fallen out. It seemed empty.

'Costa, is everything, alright?' Tracy asked, standing in front of our cabin door. I did not reply. Just then, a serious-looking man wearing a blue suit with a matching tie came marching towards us.

'Ship security,' he declared. A short young woman, dressed in white, followed him. 'Is anyone in need of medical attention?' she inquired, her head moving side-to-side, checking us out.

'I am Costa Papacosta, police captain. I am staying next door. I heard screaming and came out...'

As I spoke, the man with the thick black mustache stared at my mouth, his eyes squinted, his lips though ready to speak remained silent. His eyes travelled around, suspiciously checking everyone out. Then, he finally spoke.

'Very good, sir. Now, please step aside and let us assess the situation,' he sternly said and walked past me.

'Be careful. There is broken glass on the floor. Don't want to contaminate the crime scene, do you?'

I was used to pompous Greek men wearing suits and thinking they were an expert on pretty much everything.

He grunted slightly and entered the room on his tiptoes, his eyes never leaving the floor. The doctor came and stood beside me.

'Whose room is this?' she asked, as Mr. Security knelt down by the pool of blood.

I turned my head to the teacher sobbing behind me.

'Holly's,' the spotty-faced boy next to her replied.

'And, when did you see Holly last?' I asked.

'She left our cabin an hour ago to come and sleep,' a black-haired teen with funky green sunglasses on said, struggling with the words; her crying choking her as she spoke.

'Is she dead?' the boy on the floor asked.

'Chris!' his teacher managed to say, though she did turn to search for the expression in my eyes.

Truth be told, I doubt anyone could lose so much blood and survive. Of course, I said no such thing.

'This is Nick Pavlou, reporting,' the muscular guard spoke into his black walkie-talkie with the silver buttons. 'We have a situation in cabin 2-0-4. I am sealing it off and coming up to bridge to inform. Get the Captain, asap.'

He listened to the crackling reply as he locked the cabin's door, ignored me, nodded to the doctor and, then, turned to the teacher and said, 'come to the area behind the reception with the girl's best friends and whoever was with her last. Wait for me there. No one is to mention anything to the other pupils or teachers.'

He then turned to my direction. 'Or other passengers,' he added and marched off in the same manner in which he arrived.

I met Tracy's eyes. She wore the same amazed expression. I could almost literally hear her thoughts.

'How the hell do crimes keep finding you?'

Chapter Seven

Ioli was never one to count time. Always thinking, always on the move, she hardly paid attention to the ever-moving hands of a clock. An hour had passed and still no sign from the shoemaker. Mr. Sakis had not been in touch. His phone rang, yet no one answered. Ioli hated the wait. Her mind travelled back in time to a seven-year-old Ioli sitting in class in a rural primary school in Chania, Crete. Mr. Andreas Savvides, their math teacher, had asked them to sit totally still and quiet for a whole minute, watching the ticking of the seconds on the black-framed wall clock of their class-room. Ioli had never felt more bored. *'Did a minute really take so long to pass?'* she had thought at the time. Mr. Andreas had their attention. He proceeded with teaching his chapter of 'Math and Time'. Nearly thirty years later, and Ioli stared at the clock thinking about how slow time moved when you paid attention to it. She spat out her strawberry-flavored gum and walked over to Alexandro, who held the case file.

Ioli and Alexandro discussed the case as grandma

Sophia finally got to visit her grandson. She took the boy in her arms and stroked his full head of auburn blonde hair. Alone in the cell, they prayed together.

Valentina spent most of the hour over the phone looking for a hotel in which the two officers could stay. 'Fully booked, sorry'. Three words she repeatedly heard until finding two single rooms. Finally, a two-star hotel on the outskirts of the town had a last-minute cancellation.

Valentina declared her success with a wide smile.

'I am going to drive Mrs. Sophia home. Maybe I should drop both of you at the hotel? To freshen up, grab a bite maybe? With all good intentions, you look tired. No offense.'

'None taken,' Ioli replied, thinking how the girl was growing on her. She, also, noted that the grin on Alexandro's face had turned into a semi-flirtatious smile. 'Sounds like a good plan. We should eat and relax and regroup in an hour to go over our next steps. The girl's best friend is coming in later and then, having given her some time, we will go visit the mother. Hopefully, Mr. Sakis will be in touch by then.'

The hotel was shaped like a chunky L, making the most out of its limited space. Its rooms were simple, not that Ioli or Alexandro required more. It was chosen by tourists for its spectacular view and its vast swimming pool that seemed to connect with the sea and sky. Ioli walked past the petite receptionist and exited the glass door to the pool area, leaving Alexandro to do all the paper work. The chlorinated waters welcomed tourists of all ages looking to cool off from the scorching sun. Kids ran around their sunbathing parents, dived into the pool under the disapproving look of the never-moving lifeguard with the frappe cup glued to his right hand, and lay out on colorful and animal-shaped inflatable mattresses. Ioli tenderly rubbed her tummy as she gazed at a tall-for-his-age, dark-haired boy laughing out loud as he squirted his father with his water pistol. Around the pool, crackling speakers blared out summer hits long forgotten in the rest of the world.

'I'm heading straight for a shower. Wash away the humidity sticking to me. If that's alright with you?' Alexandro's voice pulled her out of her daydreaming about a son she had yet to meet.

Ioli turned around with a wide smile. 'You're asking for my permission to shower?'

Alexandro chuckled awkwardly. 'No, no. I meant if you don't need me at the moment...'

'It's fine. I need to lay down for a bit. My back is killing me and my feet are starting to resemble my poor grandma's.'

Again, he smiled awkwardly and not knowing how to reply, he saluted her and rushed off to his room.

Ioli gazed, once more, towards the direction of the pool, wondering if she should have taken a leave of absence. Enjoyed a week away in a nice hotel with her husband. After everything she saw during her time as a cop, Ioli often felt guilty when having a good time. Her mind seemed unable to shake out the gruesome images and allow her to relax and enjoy the finer things in life. An urge lived deep in her; an urge to help, to protect, to punish. Every now and then, she would pass the homicide department psychology's office. She would approach the door, yet had never knocked. Secretly, she hoped having a baby would bring enough joy and light to fight away the darkness in her mind and heart.

Back in her room, she showered, letting the cold water

run freely, cooling her aching body as it travelled down and circled the drain. Coming out of the bathroom, she checked the time on her phone. She set the alarm clock, which informed her she had only thirty-seven minutes to sleep, and fell backwards down on the bed. In less than a minute, she was fast asleep.

Thirty-seven minutes went by as quick as thirty-seven seconds. At least, Ioli's mind perceived it that way. Drowsily, she searched for her phone and finally, brought silence to the dark room. 'What kind of idiot named this alarm tone, Summer Bliss? What's so freaking blissful about a high-pitched beeping sound with piano in the background?' she grunted, her mouth half-buried in the uncomfortable flat pillow.

She stood up naked and began to dress. As she placed her shoes on her aching feet, Valentina called her on her phone and Alexandro knocked discreetly on the door.

'Punctual Greeks, that's a first.'

In less than ten minutes, the trio sat in the station under the cooling air provided by the powerful A/C. Valentina filled in their short wait, with retelling how she had found nothing remarkable in Mrs. Sophia's house. A clean old lady's home, tidy with icons scattered around. Adonis's room held nothing connected to the victim or the vicious murder. 'Your average teenage room it is not,' Valentina said. 'It was like two people lived in there. The posters on the walls and the dark colors indicated a young adult, yet toys were placed on the carpet, kids' comic books were stacked on the night stand...'

'His two natures. A boy in an eighteen-year-old's body,' Ioli said and once again found herself looking up at the clock. Their wait was not long.

Soon, a plethoric blonde wearing a red tank top and a black mini skirt -both a size too small, entered the station.

'Hurry up child,' she snapped, pushing her shy eighteen-year-old daughter into the room.

While her own face was ready for the ball, not an ounce of make-up covered her shy daughter's face.

'Go on, Melina. I haven't got all day. I have a speech in half-an-hour. Tell them what you told me at home and let's get going.'

As her daughter approached and sat in the chair provided to her by Alexandro, the feisty woman continued 'sorry, but it's election period and I am this island's best chance to get rid of that lazy, sleazy mayor of ours.'

Ioli did not bother with a reply. She focused her attention to the young brunette opposite her.

'Melina, right? So, officer Valentina Kokkinou informed me that Natalie was at your house last night. I just need you to confirm our timeline and then, let's talk about Natalie. I'm sure, as her best friend, you will be a great help...'

'I lied.'

'Excuse me?'

Melina could not bear Ioli's eyes and lowered her own to the floor. 'I lied. I always lie for her.' She paused, her eyes growing watery.

'Oh, come on, child, stop being so frigging sentimental. You know it's a crime keeping the truth...' her mother's rant began, before being silenced by the rise of Ioli's palm.

'Melina?' Ioli asked, leaning closer. 'It's alright, go on.'

'We were not best friends. She just let me say so and in return I lied for her. You see, I am not the most popular girl in school and Natalie's mother is way overprotective. It was a win-win situation.'

'Where was Natalie last night, then?'

The girl raised her shoulders. 'She never told me. It was with one boy or another. Though, lately, she seemed happier and when I asked her about it, she said she had finally found herself a real man and not another dumb boy.'

'What a slut. I'm so glad you're not really friends with her,' her mother commented. 'Can we go, now?'

Ioli, again, did not bother to reply. Valentina whispered to the lady to give them a little more time.

'Melina, can you think of anyone who would wish to hurt Natalie?'

At first, the girl shook her head. Then, she said 'well, Andreas was pissed off at her. They had a real big argument last month at our graduation party.'

'Andreas? Is he a classmate?' Ioli asked, remembering Adoni mentioning the name.

Melina nodded.

'What did they fight about?'

'He was her date for the dance. He was really happy that she had said yes. He was sure he was going to score, with her being so easy and all, and then, when she said no because she had a boyfriend, he went full swing mad. Called her a whore and left the party. Worst of all for him, was that both his best mates had slept with Nat during the year.'

The girl's blunt honesty was deafening. The image of the innocent young victim was fading away. However, none of her life choices meant she deserved to die and Ioli believed in justice for all.

Ioli watched as the mother and daughter rushed out of the building and went off to the gathering of Mrs. Helen's supporters.

'Being mayor in a small village is more prestigious than

winning a Nobel prize,' Valentina joked. 'Everyone pays attention to you, something all small island folk yearn for.'

'Well said,' Alexandro commented with a smile.

Ioli exhaled a silent laugh and asked about Andreas.

'He is the shoemaker's son,' Valentina said, raising her thin-line eyebrows.

Ioli's eyes opened wide. 'Really, now?'

Chapter Eight

Evening's arrival made no significant impact on the temperature and the humidity stuck to your skin worse than chewed gum on the bottom of a school chair. The shades of orange in the sky were a delight to the eye and Ioli smiled, fondly reminiscing her wedding day in the neighboring island of Santorini.

The colors around them were in full contrast to the group of black-dressed people outside Natalie's grieving mother's house. The humble garden with the crooked, faded-blue fence welcomed friends and relatives of the family that came to support Electra on the loss of her only daughter. Some wiped away tears from the corners of their eyes, some hugged, and some patted each other on the back. Most smoked. None spoke.

A well-groomed fifty-year-old with dyed black hair that fooled no-one welcomed them.

'I am Orestis Stamos, mayor of Chora. You are the officers from the mainland, right?' he asked, and continued talking without waiting for anyone's reply. 'Anything you need, do not hesitate to ask. The town council is here to support you in any manner possible,' he added, speaking louder as to be heard by the assembly behind him. They may be grieving, but they were still going to vote in the upcoming election.

'Thank you,' Ioli said, shaking his extended, golden ring wearing hand and proceeded to introduce herself and her partner.

They crossed the land of piercing eyes and reached the open front door. Inside, the smell of freshly-cooked meals lingered through the air. Greek customs never die. Everybody brought a plate, a pot or a tinfoil tray filled with food.

A young boy, not older than five, ran around in the narrow hallway filled with wooden frames that housed the course of the twins' lives in photographs. Natalie's and Gregory's most important moments unfolded before their eyes. First and last days of school. School plays. Weddings. Christenings. Sporting events. Family holidays. A wall of happiness and smiles. Electra glowed in each one, standing beside her children. It was a weird notion placing a face to the headless body left to rot upon a rooftop. A pretty girl with intense energetic eyes. You could almost see the fire in her soul. From a young age, she had make-up on, her eyebrows were carefully plucked and various colors had decorated her hair throughout the years. Ioli paused at the last framed photo that hung tilted to the left. She immediately straightened it.

The boy held a paper plane and imitating an engine sound, he cruised through the house, blissfully oblivious to the sadness surrounding him.

'Hey kid,' Ioli kneeled at his eye level. Ioli's smile and beauty always captured the attention of children who sensed her kindness and sincerity. 'That's a great plane. I'm sure you'll be a great pilot one day.'

The boy giggled and color appeared on his tender, round-as-autumn-apples cheeks. 'Where's the living room, Mr. Pilot?'

The green-eyed boy pointed to the large sliding door on the right.

Ioli knocked and the door glided open. A tall boy with tanned olive skin had his hand on the handle and his reddish eyes on Ioli. The boy from the photos.

'Gregory, my sincere condolences. I am Lieutenant Ioli Cara, Homicide division. I understand the tremendous difficulty of the hour, but I need to speak to both you and your mother.' Her eyes travelled through the room. Electra sat motionless in a worn-in purple armchair. A lady, slightly younger than she, stood behind her. The resemblance was striking.

A sister or a first cousin, for sure.

Electra's eyes were focused on Natalie's portrait on the wall opposite her. The statue of a grieving mother, Electra did not bother to turn as they entered the room.

Gregory raised his arm and with an open palm showed them to the sofa. He, also, went and stood behind his mother. The curtains were shut and only two twin lamps offered light to the gloomy room.

Ioli sat down first, her fellow two officers sitting beside her. Ioli introduced them quickly and once again offered her condolences.

'... just a few questions and we will be on our way. I respect your time of grieving and wish not to trouble you further...'

'You got her murderer. Why do you need to bother us?' Voula, Electra's sister, snapped.

'Everything needs to be put in order and every detail explored. No mistakes are in anybody's best interest. A court of law needs evidence, a timeline, a motive,' Ioli replied calmly and continued with her routine set of questions.

Voula answered all of Ioli's inquiries, confirming what they already knew. Natalie left to go to her friend's house.

She, also, contradicted popular opinion, portraying her niece as sweet and lovable. 'No, she never had a boyfriend,' her aunt proclaimed.

Ioli noticed Gregory smirk and roll his eyes. She decided not to ask any more questions and try to approach Gregory on his own. It was obvious that Natalie had managed to keep her erotic escapades a secret from her family.

'Thank you for all your help,' Ioli said, placing her right hand on the sofa's arm and lifting her growing-by-the-day body up. 'Gregory, could you escort us out, please?'

Gregory nodded, unaware of the lady cop's intentions.

Only then, did Electra speak. 'I read you, lady. If you are not sure that Adonis killed my Natalia, make sure. I want her murderer punished.'

Ioli nodded confidently and followed Gregory out of the olive-scented room. With her hand behind her back, she signalled to Valentina and Alexandro to exit the house.

'*Hopefully they will mingle with the crowd and learn something rather than flirt with each other*,' she thought, as she commented on the back garden that came into view from the kitchen door. 'What a lovely garden. Must be amazing to sit on the grass and enjoy the view. Do you mind if we step outside and sit for a while? My back is killing me.'

Ioli could not believe she would use her baby as an excuse to investigate. '*Sorry baby. Guess you are investigating, too.*'

Again, Gregory nodded reluctantly, strings of his brown hair falling in front of his too-small-for-his-face eyes.

'Erm, sure,' he replied with his deep, husky voice and scratched the back of his head. He was kind enough to pull out a white, plastic garden chair for Ioli. 'Here.'

'Thank you,' she said and sat down. The flowery scent came as a relief after sniffing the olive leaves burning inside the house in memory of the dead. The view was even more enjoyable with the winds coming alive in the evening and the colors more vivid as the sun journeyed down; ready to dip into its sea bed for the night.

'My closest childhood friends were twins,' she lied. 'It was amazing how connected they were and how they knew everything about each other.'

'Cut the crap, lady. We're on our own, now. What do you really want to know?'

'The real Natalie.'

Gregory pulled out another dirty garden chair, swung it around and sat upon it, his legs wide open and his arms resting on the chair's back. 'As if the bastards around the village haven't already bad-mouthed her.'

'What's to bad-mouth...'

'You talk a lot of crap; you know that?'

'And you're a very angry, rude young man,' Ioli replied with a smile. Gregory smiled back. 'Okay, so Natalie had a lot of boyfriends. So? It's 2016...'

'2016 where you come from! Here, we are a hundred years behind Athens. Do you know how hard it is to have Natalie as a sister in a community as small as ours?'

'And, I'm guessing you are a saint?'

'Oh come on, you're Greek. You know how it goes in villages. Guys can sleep around as much as they want and get a pat on the back for being Alpha males, while girls are labelled *poutanes*, village sluts.'

'Did she really have so many boyfriends?'

'Boyfriends! Even the word is a joke when it comes to Natalie. She had more one-night-stands than I have toes.'

Ioli leaned forward. 'And this annoyed you greatly, didn't it?'

'Shouldn't it? I am the man of the house and...'

'Is that the only reason?'

'Well, no. She could have restrained herself and kept her hands off my friends. Can you imagine being around your mates and knowing that half of them had banged your sister?'

His voice remained whispery as he did not wish to be heard in the house. However, the tone grew hostile and vile colored his words. His reddish eyes looked ready to release tears of anger.

'Anyway,' he continued, 'it's all gone now. Meaningless. Natalie is dead. And, what a death...'

He choked on the last few words. He shied away from Ioli and quickly wiped the tears forming in the corners of his eyes. 'Where is my phone?' he changed the subject. 'I keep losing that damn thing.'

'Sorry,' he excused himself as he rushed by her, into the house, seemingly searching for his phone.

Ioli leaned back and exhaled deeply. She did not get to ask the main subject on her mind. However, other thoughts -just born- preoccupied her. Her mind travelled to her reckless, teenage godson. Antony had lost three phones in less years, before his father found a way to track his phone.

Her right hand, having gently passed from the top of her forehead, taking away droplets of sweat while carefully avoiding her *neatly pulled back into a ponytail* hair, journeyed down and reached into her pocket. She brought her smart phone to eye level, flicked through her contact list, pressed dial and raised her cell to her right ear.

'Hey, pregnant lady,' Timothy's joyful, screechy voice came through the receiver. 'How's evil under the sun turning out for you and baby bump?'

'I love that you think you are funny,' she replied to her friend and best -according to most- tech genius the Hellenic force had to offer. 'I'm doing fine. Relaxing and working on my tan.'

'Fabulous as always,' he said, and ended the sentence with a giggle. 'Now, who is trying to be funny? So, what do you need?'

'Who said I need something?'

'I'm listening.'

'Can you trace the location of a phone for me?'

'Sure. Provider?'

'Erm, not sure...'

'No prob. Give me the number.'

'Give me a sec,' Ioli said, lowering her phone and searching in her left pocket for her mini note pad. She flicked through the pages with the many scribbles, thinking how her nails looked awful. Faded and scraped-off nail polish coated her unevenly cut nails. One was even chipped on the end.

'Okay, you ready?'

'Girl, I was born ready.'

'Cool it, Coolio,' she laughed and proceeded to list the number belonging to Mr. Sakis, the shoe-repair man who had not been in-touch since his phone call to the station's answering machine.

'Give me a few minutes. How's Mark, the dreamy doctor doing?'

'He's fine. Anxious about becoming a father. How's your dreamy man?'

'Stefano is anxious about moving in with me. He keeps calling it the next important step in our relationship. Men!'

Ioli laughed quietly. 'Listen, I'll call you back. Have to get this question out of my head.'

'Kisses,' he replied and hung-up.

Ioli re-entered the house and crossed the empty hallway. She reached three doors. She guessed that the door with the ENTER-AT-YOUR-OWN-RISK blue sign was Gregory's bedroom.

Ioli knocked and having received no reply, she counted to five and pulled down on the scratched door knob. Gregory turned his head and with his eyebrows raised, he stared at Ioli. This time he did not bother hiding his tears.

'I know, I am being intrusive, I will leave, just answer me this. Did Natalie talk to you about her new boyfriend? Her friend mentioned...'

'Talk to *me?*' he mocked the word. 'Natalie did not tell people shit. But, last week when I confronted her, having caught her creeping in through the kitchen window again, she told me to stay out of her way and that she was having the time of her life. I asked what was so different about her new addition to her long list of lovers and she replied he's rich. Rolex, suit and tie rich,' he said as he stood up and closed his door. 'Please, don't let mother know any of this. Natalie is gone, now. No reason for her to know the true nature of her daughter.'

Ioli felt the need to place her hand on his shoulder, to offer him a sympathetic smile or a similar gesture, yet she controlled the urge. As much as she wished to succour the young man, his anger and his love for his mother earned him a place on Ioli's suspect list.

Chapter Nine

Five years ago, Mr. and Mrs. Jones from Canterbury, Kent decided that at age sixty and having worked their grocery shop for forty years, it was time to retire.

'We're not getting any younger and we are stuck here in this shop for fourteen hours a day. I want out. I want to live for us. Somewhere nice, exotic. Set off on a new adventure,' Bertha tried once again to persuade her stubborn-headed, high school sweetheart, Oliver.

'What about the kids?' he replied, stacking the day's freshly-arrived tomatoes.

'Now, that's a *new* excuse from you,' she laughed. 'The *kids* are thirty-five years old and live hours away. We would always come and visit, and better, they would love to come visit us.'

Oliver stood up straight and stared at his wife with her rosy cheeks and her curly, brown hair. Those eyes always had a way with him. 'Where? And don't you dare say Benidorm!'

Bertha's eyes lit up as she skipped through the rows of

vegetables towards him. Her mouth reached speeds, never before witnessed by Oliver.

'I was thinking somewhere in the Mediterranean. An Italian or Greek island. Somewhere really quiet, like a village where we would sit in the garden all day soaking up the sun, reading our books, dipping in our own private pool, making love...'

'Bertha!' Oliver cut her flow of words as his head spun around to make sure there were no customers in the shop.

'Come on, old man! Let's sell up and leave,' she said and placed a full-lip kiss on his ready-to-speak lips.

Bertha recalled that day as she sat on her favorite blue deck chair staring at the lowering sun from her garden, right next to the 200-meter cliff. Oliver lay on his inflatable bed, his hands and legs dipped in the pool.

'What's all the racket?' Oliver grunted.

'Racket! I wonder what you would say if there was really a commotion going on. It's some people with that police officer looking around.'

'Looking for what?'

'How should I know?' she asked as she watched Ioli traipse up and down the road glancing around.

Valentina had already started to knock on neighbors' doors asking if they had seen Mr. Sakis.

Alexandro had his head over a stone brick wall that was built around an area of green, looking among pine trees and small-flowered tamarisks; planted and taken care of by the village council as the crooked, wooden sign informed.

'Are you sure?' Ioli asked over the phone.

'For the millionth of time, babe, yes,' Timothy replied, his eyes glued to his computer screen watching the red blinking dot of Mr. Sakis' phone. 'I haven't got the four clear signals that I normally need, but he should be around twelve to twenty meters from you.'

'Maybe he dumped his phone,' Ioli replied, her head scanning over a faded-yellow, public trash can. 'Call you back,' she said and closed her phone. She looked straight ahead at the plump lady standing at her shiny white fence between short bushes filled with colorful roses. The lady with the black swimsuit watched as she walked towards her.

'Good evening,' Ioli called over and began to introduce herself.

'Bertha,' the woman replied sweetly extending her hand. 'What is this all about?'

'We are looking for Mr. Sakis, the shoe repair man, if you know him.'

'Oh, yes. The kind gentleman with the beard. Is he missing? I thought you were here for the murder of that poor young girl,' Bertha said, placing her hand on her cheek. Her lips travelled down and a cloud of sorrow lingered across her hazelnut eyes.

'We are,' Ioli replied, leaning on the fence. 'How long have you been in Folegandros?' Ioli asked, wondering if she was wasting her time on a tourist renting for the summer.

'Oh, five years today, actually. Such a lovely place, really. Heaven on earth, this weather. I grew up in the rain, you see.'

'And the people?'

'Everyone is so lovely here. Amazing characters. Don't let this murder fool you. It's a safe place...'

'Bull,' Oliver's gravelly voice came from behind her. 'If you listen to my wife, you would believe everybody was a saint.'

'And, you sir, don't believe so? About the islanders, I mean.'

'There are some good folk, of course,' he replied, coming closer and standing next to his wife. Ioli's eyes travelled along his bare chest and arms, admiring his multiple tattoos. 'But, they have this small village mentality. They all have a great idea about themselves and talk about others all day. The stories, you hear! If you believe them all true, there is something sinister about every single one of them.'

'Even Adonis?'

'The special needs' kid who broke people's windows by throwing rocks at whomever made fun of him?' Oliver replied, sarcasm coloring his words.

'Oh, Oliver. Stop being so grumpy,' his wife told him off.

'And, Natalie?' Ioli asked, glad to have found someone with pure honesty.

'Poor girl,' Bertha said loudly as her husband opened his mouth. 'Let's not bad-mouth the dead.'

Neither her words nor her hand around Oliver's wrist could contain her husband's words.

'She had it coming, if you ask me. Would sleep with the whole island if she could...'

'Oliver!'

'What? You're forgetting the night we came home and caught her in our pool having sex.'

'With whom?' Ioli interrupted their locked together eyes.

'Some tourist. Definitely not from around here,' Oliver answered. 'Anyway, you caught the guy. Why are you going around house to house?'

'They are looking for Mr. Sakis, the shoe guy?' his wife informed him.

Oliver raised his thick grey eyebrows. 'Wow, two crimes in a day. What is this island coming to?' he said and chuck-

71

led. 'Good luck, Miss Lieutenant,' he said and began walking back to his pool.

'Are you sure, dear, that he was last seen here?' Bertha asked, her fingers interlocked, her eyes sorry for the pregnant lady in despair.

'Our computer says his phone is around here.'

'Check the caldera,' Oliver said, diving into the serene waters of his swimming pool.

'Oliver,' his wife told him off once more.

'What?' he replied, coming to the surface. 'That drunk fell over his own feet.'

Ioli's eyes widened. She approached the half-meter wall that run along the steep drop. She placed her hands on the wall and keeping her baby in mind, leaned over, her eyes scanning the rocky ground below.

There, among cans of coke and dried up shrubs lay a man's body.

'Guys,' she called over to her fellow police officers. Both ran to her side. Both stood staring in shock down at the human figure with the spread out arms and legs below.

'Is it Mr .Sakis?' Alexandro asked, turning his head to Valentina.

'Hard to tell from this high up.'

'Open and shut case, for fuck's sake!' Ioli said and asked how to get down there.

Chapter Ten

ON BOARD

Mrs. Anne advised the children to remain calm and left them in the care of her fellow teacher, Mr. Zack, short for Zachariah. A large sixty-year-old with a bored expression and a passion for silence; he had once said that people should have a limited word limit throughout the day. One wondered how he taught Science and Chemistry at the prestigious International School of Athens. Mrs. Anne's advice calmed no one, not even herself. Panting and with an inner *nerve earthquake*, she followed Nick, the security guy and Katerina, the ship's doctor, up to the bridge.

Nick's expression changed midway; his still, tough expression gave way to a worried look. His strong jaw moved around as his teeth rubbed against each other. Katerina's hand slowly drifted into his huge hands and she caressed his fingers. He turned and tilted his head downwards to lock into his *two feet shorter than him* girlfriend.

'I'm okay.'

'I know. I just want you to know that I am here,' Katerina said, giving her best shot at a compassionate smile.

73

Katerina has seen her fair share of blood. A Doctor Without Borders and a daredevil by nature, she spent most of her after-uni years in poverty-ridden countries and war zones. Dead children during the Syrian conflict is where her soul drew the line. Too young, too many. Katerina found herself not being able to even work in an E.R.. Private practice was out of the question. The fourth child from a poor family and with a huge college debt, the last thing Katerina needed was more loans. The job description for a doctor on board a ship for the 'well-off' -as she referred to the passengers of the reputable liner- sounded heavenly made. Her third year upon board and she had helped senior couples with their medications, tied a young boy's leg and fought tricky fevers; and those were the hard cases. Mostly, she did nothing more than a nurse in her first year of training. And that suited Katerina just fine.

Outside the sealed-off cabin, I read the eyes of the group of teens before me .

'Who was her roommate?' I asked.

'That would be me, sir,' an athletic girl in a short black skirt and a red bikini top, replied in a southern American accent.

'And you are?'

'Nicole. Nicole Winthrop,' she answered, waiting for the set of detective questions to commence. TV shows had made everyone an expert, yet she did not expect the next question.

'Where was the vase placed?'

Nicole's eyes flicked faster than usual. 'Err, I think it was on the bedside table.'

'You think?' I asked, my eyes steady on her.

'No, no. I'm sure.'

I turned and put my hand through the X-shaped tape

that Nick Pavlou had placed across the door. I pushed the door open and ducked below the *slightly moving from the air-conditioning* tape. I looked down at the smashed vase and bit my bottom lip, lost in thought. Carefully, I approached the jewelry box. I flicked it, turning it around, making sure I did not touch it. A piece of ribbed paper lay under it. I took out my cell and with my sausage fingers, took a while to zoom-in and take a decent picture of the writing. With one last look around the room, I exited into the hall and closed the door behind me. The science teacher had already ordered the group of teens to follow him to the cafeteria on the front deck.

'Ice-cream and fresh sea air for all,' he said and added a strong 'come on' at the reluctant to move, numb minors.

I returned to my cabin to find Tracy sitting on one of the two chairs of our petite balcony. 'You disappeared quickly.'

'I knew your investigating inner self would surface. Scan the crime scene and questioned the witnesses, have we?' she asked, taking a long sip from her frozen pina-colada. Her larger-than-life straw hat with the pink ribbon traveling around her head, made it hard to read her face. But, I knew my wife's tone well. She was in high spirits. It was needless to excuse myself from switching from romantic Costa to homicide division Costa, as Tracy understood that a good mystery would work better wonders on me than all the sea air, mighty sun and relaxing would ever do.

'Where's my glasses?' I asked the second most common question of our marriage. The first being 'what's for dinner?'. Weddings are basically two people asking each other what to eat until one of the two dies.

'Give me the phone,' she said, stretching out her hand. 'I can't be bothered to explain to you in detail where your glasses are, only for you to lose your temper and move everything around in our luggage and still not find them. Now, there's a mystery for you. How can you solve murder cases based on the slightest clue or small piece of seemingly unimportant evidence yet can't find something in my bag or drawer.'

'Finished?'

'Just pass me the phone.'

Tracy zoomed into the photo ably and began to read.

'I question their judgmental glares as I wonder, what have I done wrong? Then, there's an ellipsis and it continues with my heart, my head, my body, numb.'

'It looks like a girl's neat handwriting. Could be the victims. Could be hers...' I began uttering my thoughts. 'Babe, google it, please. Could be a known poem or something. For her to use an ellipsis, could be an entire poem...'

'Izzy Dix. It's a poem about bullying,' my internet-friendly wife interrupted me.

I placed my hands on the blue railing and gazed out into the endless shades of blue. 'Did she leave it there on purpose? Was it just something she kept in her jewelry box? I think I have to talk to her teacher,' I finally spoke.

'Her boyfriend would know more,' Tracy said and picked up her Lynda Le Plante book. Tracy had fallen in love with the British crime books featuring Anna Travis. I don't think she felt as warmly towards my idea of investigating the pool of blood next door.

Chapter Eleven

The sun opposite her had begun its unrushed, leisurely dive into the glassy ocean. Multiple shades of fiery red and dark orange swam upon the short-lived waves. Ioli sat on the protecting-from-the-cliff wall and stared down at the body.

Neither option of approaching the dead man seemed sensible for a pregnant lady. Drive to the nearest point possible and hike along the steep rocks or take a boat to the shore opposite the body and walk through dried-up fields. Alexandro and Valentina had opted for the second option.

Ioli had just called her husband and reluctantly informed him that she would be spending the night on the island. She believed she did a good job persuading him not to worry.

'Come on, baby. You could even bring your girlfriend around,' she joked, interrupting his flow of angry words.

'Don't. Don't color this funny. You are...'

'Okay, okay. No girlfriend. How about pizza, beer and finally watching the latest two episodes of Game of Thrones you never have time to see?'

'That's more like it,' he had replied, calmer than before.

Ioli rubbed her belly as she straightened her posture; her legs hanging from the wall, brought much needed relief to her feet. Her mind pictured Mark's night in. Being married -and happily married, too- still had not sunk in. She was never the one for relationships. Having dedicated most of her adult life to her job, Mark was her life's fourth relationship, counting her innocent high school crush.

'Excuse me, love. Would you fancy a cup of tea?' Bertha's soothing voice cut her life's movie, playing in the amphitheatre of her mind.

Ioli turned her head to reply, her loose black hair suffering from the humidity and the heat. 'I think I'd have a heartburn if I drunk anything hot in this weather.'

Bertha laughed and her whole body danced along with the hearty laughter.

'Typical Greek. I'll get you some icy rose water, then.'

'That's more like it. Thank you,' Ioli replied, as the merry woman bobbled into her well-maintained bungalow.

'I'll have a cuppa, dear,' her husband yelled from the refreshing chlorinated waters in which he swam; a curious grin on his face as he watched the fishing boat carrying the two young officers approach the uninhabited, unfriendly shore below.

'Be careful,' the boat's captain advised as he lowered his wooden, hand-made bridge to the dark sands. Only a quarter of the sun remained above sea level.

'Here, take my hand,' Alexandro said, extending his right arm.

The corners of Valentina's red lips travelled slightly upwards as she placed her hand into his. Soon, both had their shoes upon the muddy land. Both waved to Ioli, settled like an eagle, watching from above.

Ioli waved back and once again got lost in thought.

'*Adonis breaking a few windows does not necessarily mean he has a mean streak. It doesn't mean he hasn't one either. Did she push him too far? Fingerprints from the scene haven't come in yet, but his fingerprints were all over his own knife. Then again, I don't trust her brother. I still have to talk to Andreas, the rejected boyfriend and find out who her new, rich boyfriend is...*'

Just then, she tried to pull out of memory her hand shake with the mayor. Flashbacks from hours ago came to life in her mind. She kept on playing the handshake in her mind. It glowed in her eyes. His golden watch.

She lowered herself from the wall, her hands steady on the dusty ledge. She rushed over to the concrete miniature roundabout that most cars chose to ignore and drove over, and stood in the center. Opposite her was the end of the garden belonging to the island's biggest villa. A circular, well-maintained, short lawn, surrounded by flower beds filled with defiant lilies and statues of Greek gods, ran all the way like an expensive carpet up to the row of palm trees that towered over the stone wall. A wall that on its outer side housed a huge poster of its owner. A poster declaring the candidacy of Orestis Stamos, mayor of Folegandros. A wrinkle-less man with shiny white teeth -both thanks to Photoshop, stood proudly in front of Ioli. Her eyes were not focused on his face, though, but on the wrist of his right arm.

'*A golden Rolex.*'

The air-piercing, loud horn made her jump back as the white car zoomed by her.

'Watch it, lady,' the shirtless, hairy driver shouted over the golden hits playing out from his open window.

Ioli raised her hand in signal of apologizing, realizing she was walking in the middle of the newly-created asphalt road. The street lights had yet to be turned on and the sunlight was weak.

'Guess this is the luck my grandma always says I have, due to her blessings,' she muttered to herself.

'Dear? Your drink?' Bertha called over as Valentina and Alexandro reached the crime scene below.

Valentina paused meters away from the lifeless bloody body.

Alexandro watched in disgust as two cats sat upon the mangled man, one drinking blood from the hanging left leg, the other biting into his exposed brains.

'Shoo, get! Off you go,' he yelled and clapped his hands, stomping towards the body with the limbs spread out in awkward angles.

'What a drop,' he said and whistled in amazement as he stared upwards, his eyes following the great expanse to the top. 'Hmm, where's Ioli?' he wondered.

He knelt down to the pallid face that had become one with the once-silvery rock. 'Is it Mr. Sakis?' he asked, only then noticing that Valentina had not moved from the spot in which she had frozen. 'What's wrong? The cats are gone. Boy, what a sight...'

'It... It's not the cats. I... I have never seen a dead body this close and in this kind of bloody situation before. Natalie was my first body. I couldn't even go near her,' she breathlessly replied, her hands slightly shaking, her eyes fixed upon the milky eyes staring blankly. 'It's him, by the way,' she managed to add, before beginning to gag. She turned her back to Alexandro and lowered her head, talking to herself to control it. Nothing disgusted her more than vomit and she was not ready to lose her club sandwich lunch.

'I'm sorry, I did not think...'

'Why would you? You are used to professionals, not silly

asses like me that have no job being on a homicide case...'
More gagging interrupted her sentence.

'Don't say that,' Alexandro replied, rushing to her side,
placing his hand upon her quivering shoulder. 'I'm the idiot.
I never stopped to think this was your first murder case. I
swear, no one is comfortable around their first dead bodies.
You are doing so much better than I was. I stepped all over
the evidence, I vomited my lunch and as the medical examiner lifted up the body and blood poured out, I fainted! I
swear to God, in front of everyone, my eyes went blank and
I...'

Valentina turned towards him and interrupted his fast
production of sympathy speech by placing a gentle kiss on
his moving lips. As the last ray of sun ran between them and
darkness surrounded them, their lips interlocked. Alexandro
was never one to miss an opportunity, dead body or not. He
placed his right hand through her bleached blond hair and
kissed her passionately. Valentina pushed him away and
took a clumsy step back.

'And I continue being a fool. God, I am so unprofessional. I do apologize, you were just trying to cheer me up
and I kissed you, and you probably have a girlfriend or two
back home...'

'You're no fool in my eyes,' Alexandro replied, beaming
proudly about how smooth he thought he was.

Valentina took her flashlight into her hands and shone
light over the area. 'Let's get to the body before we can't
even see our noses out here.'

'You're right,' Alexandro agreed, lighting up his flashlight and approaching the victim, careful not to step on
pieces of brain and bone particles. 'Man, what a drop,' he
said and whistled. 'I'll collect whatever I can,' he said,
taking out of his backpack a roll of plastic evidence bags.

'Then, I'll bag the body. I think you should go get the captain to help us carry him.'

Above, Ioli had placed her cold beverage upon the sand-covered wall. Her dry lips had welcomed the icy rose water and it even helped with the dizziness she was feeling. She watched as the two dots below turned on their lights and approached the bloody omelette that was once Mr. Sakis. She finished off her beverage slowly, her eyes following the cadaver as it was bagged and carried to the boat.

She took the empty glass back to Mrs. Bertha and thanked her.

'Was it the shoe maker, then?' Oliver asked, standing behind his wife, drying himself with a rather small for his size, Scooby-Doo towel.

'Good night, Mr. Oliver,' Ioli nodded and began to walk towards the center of town.

'Ooh, mysterious,' he mocked, and lifted his fingers into the air, mimicking spooky wind with an expression of comical shock drawn upon his aging face.

'Grow up, Oliver,' Bertha retorted and pushed him towards the house. 'Go, get. Stop embarrassing me.'

Ioli did not hear Bertha's ongoing rumbling as she took her phone with the Westeros cover out her pocket and called Alexandro.

'Don't bother coming to pick me up. I'll walk back to the station...'

'You sure, boss? I...'

'I'm pregnant, not disabled and please don't interrupt me,' Ioli replied with a strong steady voice. 'By the time the boat docks and you get the body to the car and then go to the station, I'll be there,' she added and lowered the phone to end the call.

'Sorry. I just...' she heard Alexandro's mellow voice. She

could picture him with his goofy look and his puppy eyes apologizing. She raised the phone back up to her ear.

'Mama always said be a gentleman, especially to ladies, especially to the elder and pregnant ones...'

'Boy, do you ever stop talking? No need to apologize. It's just my hormones...' she began to say before regretting the lie and pausing. 'That's no excuse. I'm sorry for being a bitch. On the bright side, there's nothing you can do about it, so get used to it,' she continued and Alexandro would swear he could feel her sense of humor in her tone.

Ioli placed her cell back into her pocket and walked along the narrow pavement beneath dim street lights and among a scent of freshly bloomed jasmine flowers that hung along many blue-painted wooden fences. The serenity of the idyllic location came to an end as she turned onto the main street and found herself in the middle of hundreds of locals leaving yet another campaign speech of Mayor Stamos.

Faces of all ages smiled at her as they passed beside her. Others looked on while others whispered who she was and proceeded to give their *expert* opinion surrounding the murder to whomever was willing to listen. Ioli offered flat smiles in return as she made her way to the fiberglass podium, placed on the highest step of the town hall's entrance. Oresti Stamos stood tall and proud, his hand around a stunning, young girl -not older than twenty. Her wide, full lipped smile, her Roman nose, her almond-shaped eyes; Ioli noticed at once that she was related to Stamos, most likely his daughter.

'*No wife?*' she thought as she confidently went up the marble steps. She waited for the clicks to die down. Two photographers, in all, and they took multiple shots from multiple angles.

'Mr. Stamos?'

Oresti Stamos turned and kept smiling widely. 'Oh, Mrs. Cara. Taking time off the case to listen to election speeches?'

Ioli flashed a full-teeth, short-lived, fake smile and replied that she had just arrived. 'I need a moment of your time. You did mention the mayor and the town hall were at our disposal...'

'Of course, of course,' he replied, placing his hand upon her back and walking her away from the remaining few of his campaign gathering. 'How is the investigation coming along? Form your case against Adonis, yet?'

'Was your daughter their classmate?'

Ioli's question caught him off guard. 'I... I... Yes, but what does that have to do with anything?'

'Oh, nothing. She just seemed the right age and I know how small schools go. Same age, same class.'

Stamos nodded in agreement, his eyes still confused on what the police lieutenant standing opposite him wanted. 'How may I be of assistance?'

Ioli ignored the question and continued her path of questioning. 'She seems like such a lovely girl. Were the two friends? With Natalie, I mean?'

'Erm, yes. I believe so.'

'Believe? You're not sure? She never came around to your house? Did *you* ever meet the deceased girl?' Ioli threw multiple questions together, her tactic of getting answers from confused minds.

'What has this...,' he replied, his eyes scanning around to check that Ioli's words only reached his pair of ears. 'Am I being interrogated here? Cause it sure feels like it,' he continued and jokingly loosened his tie and pulled on his beige shirt's collar.

'*Joke or not, you need to let your tie free. You are flushed, Mr. Mayor.*'

'Of course not. I know how small islands can be and I know the mayor knows much about the people of his town. So, what can you tell me about Natalie? How was she when she came around to your house...' Ioli paused to read his expression and continued, 'to see your daughter?'

'Kind girl. Kind girl. Always smiling. Beautiful and polite. Such a shame.'

Ioli felt she was watching a cheesy, Latin soap-opera performance. At least, she confirmed that he knew Natalie and that she visited his house.

'Who knew Adonis had it in him?!'

'Hmm, yes,' Ioli replied and nodded. 'And, where was your daughter last night?' she asked, watching his eyes open wide while his trimmed eyebrows turned into facial rainbows. 'You see, Natalie was not where her mother believed her to be and we have to check with her friends about possible whereabouts.'

'My daughter was at her aunt's watching a movie with her cousins. They were not that close, I doubt she would know where Natalie was.'

'Out for the night, then. And, you?'

'And me, what?' he asked, crossing his arms across his broad chest.

'Home alone? I don't see a Mrs. Stamos...'

'My wife is away on business. She maintains a law office in Naxos. She takes on cases across the Cyclades... You know, I'd like to know what you are getting at, lady...' he said, whispering angrily, his hands lowering, coming to his side, both clenched together in fists. His Rolex watch and his gold bracelet rattled as he moved.

'A bit of a temper you got there, mayor.'

Ioli remained still as he stepped closer. 'I am a very peaceful man. I do not like being provoked and election season is very stressful. That wretched Helen is gaining voters by the day. I love my island and I need another term to make all my dreams for this island come true. Folegandros is slowly becoming a dynamic tourist destination with nothing to be jealous of, by Mykonos and Santorini...'

'Save your passionate election speeches for people who vote here, Mr. Stamos. Temper and stress combined with the possible gossip of an affair with an eighteen-year-old girl... whoo,' Ioli said, exhaling deeply at the end. 'Now, that's a lot of heat, hotter than this damn heatwave.'

The mayor's breathing became louder and his hands once again formed fists. 'You believe these idiots that have nothing better to do than talk shit about me? Get serious, lady...'

'Call me *lady* one more time and I will make sure that that *shit* you claim becomes common knowledge around here.'

'You have some nerve. Our police have arrested the guilty party. Pack your bags. I'm calling your supervisor and complaining about your attitude and for harassing me with stupid accusations...'

'Accusations to which you haven't provided an answer. I saw your face outside her mother's house and that sorrow was not from losing a precious voter. Natalie talked about you. You and your Rolex. Sleep tight, Mayor. Our paths will surely cross soon.'

Mr. Stamos shook his head, his thick, short-cut beard swung side to side. His hands relaxed, his eyes returned to their normal color and size and he blew out air. 'You've got it all wrong, Lieutenant. We are a peaceful, loving community with good, old family values. Just because a kid whose brain does not allow him to know better committed such a terrible crime, does not mean you get to accuse us for all the sins in the book.' It was the first time Ioli felt she was hearing his true voice. Not his mayor's voice, not his macho voice nor his angry voice.

'How wonderful you make everything sound. But you know what Mr. Stamos? You could take a pile of shit and call it chocolate pie, yet it will still be crap. There's been another murder. Your island is not as innocent as you paint it to be. If Adonis is guilty of killing Natalie, then it would seem like you have another killer on the loose. Or maybe, the real first killer is covering up his tracks? Maybe a lover with too much to lose... like an important upcoming election.'

All of Mr. Stamos's facial muscles took the route of gravity as he mumbled a question about who had died. Ioli had already turned around and began walking back to the police station. She knew well that he would not risk talking louder or following her for answers as dozens of potential voters still lingered in the picturesque square.

While Ioli quickened her pace and opened a little bag of cute, colorful Gummy bears, trying to shake off the adrenaline rush of her heated discussion with the mayor, the wooden fishing boat with the faded, chipped paint arrived in the peaceful bay of Karavostasi. Upon it, was the chain-smoking, in his late eighties sea captain, Alexandro, Valentina and a body bag with what remained of the shoemaker's corpse. Not all of him could be scraped off the rocks.

Alexandro had just gotten off the phone with Dr. Jacob, the coroner. He informed him that they had another body and that they would be requiring a clean-up crew for the scene on the rocks below the caldera. Multiple curse words came through the receiver, all being muffled by the chicken sandwich being devoured by the medical examiner at that moment. 'I hell am not coming out in the heat tomorrow to collect another body. And, I don't care if God himself asks me to do it, I surely am not going to collect pieces of tissue and shit off rocks below the fucking cliff. I'll send out a team of rookies. Practice makes perfect, my boy,' he added, somewhat more calmly than his first reaction. 'By the way, I have sent my initial report via the station's fax. Nothing really exciting, but Ioli's mind has the ability to produce results from the smallest details. Oh, and the lab sent their report, too. None of the fingerprints lifted from the roof matched Adonis or any other set in the system,' the chatty doctor continued and then hung up without waiting for a reply to anything he had just said.

'Wow, that guy can talk fast. More than your average Greek,' Alexandro said, tucking his phone into his front pocket. 'Unlike you, whose tongue has been kidnapped by an island street cat,' he said after a short pause. Valentina sat silently on a nailed-to-the-deck, ready-to-crumble-into-pieces bench, her eyes following the pacific waves moving endlessly towards the moonlight.

'Huh? Yeah, yeah. You're right. He talks too much,' she mumbled as she saw him staring at her and turned her eyes away.

'I enjoyed our...' he began to say. Alexandro pondered if she could not hear him clearly due to the feverish howling of the wind or if she was ignoring him. His instincts drove him to the latter.

'I really did enjoy our kiss...' he said, this time sitting right next to the quiet woman.

'Oh, my God. Seriously? This is the time to talk about it? As we are going to unload a splattered dead guy and throw him into the back of my car? I already feel like a fool, please do not add *utter idiot* to the list. This is unprofessional and...'

'And I thought the coroner talked speedily,' he said and chuckled in anticipation if it was one of the times his humor alone would save him.

'Please, don't joke.'

'Please, don't let all the shit around us stop us from getting to know each other.'

He placed his waxed hand upon hers- Alexandro never shied away from being a new age metrosexual guy, he waxed all his upper body and even shaved his Greek hairy legs during the shorts-wearing summer. Her hand was cold, frozen-food cold.

'I know, it was a spur of the moment kiss, and yes, out of place and under our working-circumstances, a bit out of order, but aren't those the fun moments in life? I truly do find you interesting, and beautiful and I would love to get to know you better after all this is done with.'

Valentina smiled for a second upon hearing his compliments, then, her lips travelled down and she pulled back her hand. 'Bet a sweet-talker like you gets to bed a lot of girls in the big city. I might have dreams of getting off this tiny rock and going somewhere big, but my values will always remain those of a small village girl. No way I'm sleeping with a guy that's here on the island for three days -tops.'

Alexandro sat up straight. 'Wait, who said anything about... You're surely rushing ahead. I said nothing about... You are judging me based solely on stereotypes. Just because you have been burnt in the past...'

Valentina stood up and walked to the railing, watching as the boat floated sideways and hit the dock.

'What past? You know nothing about girls like me.

Guess you don't have any twenty-six-year old virgins in Athens, huh?' she asked and hopped off the boat.

The dock was quiet. Only swarms of mosquitoes buzzing around the lamp posts and a pair of old sea dogs fishing on its end, their aging feet and rods hanging from the pier. A perfect time to carry a body bag and avoid gossip which in small island communities, spreads faster than wild-fire in dried up grass.

'Back seat or boot?' asked the English-Greek Captain who had long regretted agreeing to taking the two officers to pick up a dead body. The only dead things he was used to carrying down the dock, were fish and octopuses.

Valentina paused for a second. The trunk seemed disgraceful while the back seat of her car gave her the chills. It did not seem like a healthy option either in her Dettol-wiped back seats. 'Trunk?'

The two men were sweating from every skin pore possible. Neither argued nor agreed. Alexandro popped open the trunk and in Mr. Sakis went.

Neither spoke during the ride back to Chora. Alexandro knew very well from experience when a woman did not want to hear another word. The stressful situation was not helping him either. He would win her over gradually.

'*A Greek hunter never gives up*,' he thought, and his trade-mark grin came to life as he felt like an alpha male.

Chapter Twelve

Ioli slowed down her pace. As her heart rate returned to more normal beats per minute, her brain started registering the aches from her swollen feet, her sore lower back and an unexplained, aggressive migraine. She turned right by the local post office and paused to catch her breath. Just then did she realize her surroundings. To one side every little street ran to the caldera, revealing a magnificent view of the moon travelling above the lit up Aegean sea, while to her other side, the narrow roads ran to the town square, where under dozens of lights hanging from tree to tree, locals and tourists enjoyed fine Greek dishes and local wines. The magical sounds from the band playing added to the ideal night out.

'*Mark would love it here,*' she thought of her quiet introverted husband. The doctor loved small, quiet, simple environments. The big city did not suit him well. Like Ioli he was a proud Cretan raised in a scenic village, among the rough lands of Crete. Ioli, whose love for her job helped her bare the difficulties of the big city, often feared that with a baby on the way, Mark would propose to return to their island.

'Maybe one day, definitely not now.'

She hardly noticed that she had begun walking again. Lost in thought, she reached the century-old building with the Corinthian entrance, also known as the Folegandros police station.

Her eyes went from the empty parking lot to Mrs. Sophia sitting patiently on the doorstep, two plastic shopping bags by her side. Her hair danced in the night breeze coming down from the north and shone silver under the moonlight. Shadows travelled across her deeply wrinkled face as she slightly rocked back and forth, moving in and out of the light.

'Good evening, Mrs. Sophia,' Ioli said, approaching her, hoping that Valentina would return soon to handle Adonis's grandmother. She had to inform Mr. Sakis's wife and question their son about his relationship with Natalie and his whereabouts at the time of her murder.

'Good evening, dear. Hope you don't mind, I brought some chicken and peas for Adonis. Valentina probably fed him a kebab like she does with the tourists or local hooligans, she has had spending the night here. His mother used to feed him takeaway crap all the time. I always cook for him,' she said, standing up with difficulty. 'I, also, brought him his pyjamas and his night light. I saw there was a plug in that hole of a room,' she added, picking up the bags.

'Come in,' Ioli replied, not commenting on all the old lady had to say. Thankfully, Valentina had given her the spare key to the heavy door. Ioli's left hand ran up the wall in search of the light switch. As soon as light spread out into the cavernous room, Ioli noticed the packet of straws lying next to the coffee machine. Ioli walked over and straightened it, tidying the jars of coffee and sugar in a row. She knew she would not be able to concentrate with the messy shelf staring at her.

'Sit down for a moment,' Ioli said, patting the old-fashioned armchair as she walked past it. She went straight for Valentina's pine-wood desk in search for the holding room key. Ioli cringed at the officer's notes. All neat and tidy with little hearts above the I's and suns sketched in the corners of the pages.

'Another hopeless romantic.'

'What's that, dear?' Mrs. Sophia asked, having just managed to settle down in the soft-backed armchair; her pitch black dress in pure contrast to the purple chair with the golden lines.

'Nothing, just talking to myself,' Ioli replied, speaking louder this time. She had just discovered the key in the second drawer when she noticed the paper sitting in the fax tray with Athens Metropolitan Police logo printed on top. *'Jacob's report.'*

'I used to talk to myself, too. A lot back in the days, after I lost my husband. I would go over again and again how to help my daughter with her drug addiction. My heart broke at the thought of Adonis being with her. But, God always finds a way. I know it's a horrible thing for a mother to say, but her death was mercy to us all. To herself, too. She was beyond saving. Only the Lord could save her from her sinful ways. Adonis grew up happy with me here. He is such a kind soul...'

Mrs. Sophia continued with a breaking voice, her usual praise for Adonis. Ioli listened and nodded, throwing in the occasional aha between her nods. Her eyes ran down the medical examiner's report.

'... *time of death: between midnight and two o'clock... death resulted due to extensive blood loss... first stabs to her back... signs of intercourse (nothing violent)... stabs to her thighs and genitalia were post mortem as was the cutting off of her breasts and beheading... contents of stomach: pork and vegetables... took a blood sample, will take days to get back results for a full tox...'*

Ioli nodded again as Mrs. Sophia retold the story how Adonis gave half his sandwich to a classmate whose mother forgot to pack him any lunch.

'What kind of mother forgets to pack her child something to eat?' Mrs. Sophia asked, raising her hands into the air. She, then crossed herself and prayed to the Virgin Mary to provide sense to all the mothers of the world.

Her prayer was cut short as she immediately leaped out of the chair upon hearing Ioli unlocking the cell and pulling open the hefty door.

'Oh, my... eh, sorry,' Ioli managed to say, her pupils dilated as she stepped back and turned away. Mrs. Sophia had somehow rushed to the door and popped her head into the room.

'I'm sorry, dear,' she said, placing her rough, wrinkled hand upon Ioli's shoulder. 'He gets nervous and he does not know better. I'll get the mop.'

Adonis stopped masturbating upon hearing his grandma's voice and quickly pulled up his shorts. He curled up in the corner of the bunk bed, his head between his legs. Semen and vomit were on the floor in front of the bed.

'No need for that, Mrs. Sophia,' Ioli said, catching her breath. 'I'm sure we can call the cleaning lady to come in...'

Mrs. Sophia's loud sardonic laughter filled the room. 'Oh, dear, you think the station has a cleaning lady? Valentina cleans it herself -and between us, not very well. She keeps daydreaming about leaving the island. No, no. That hair, those nails. She won't clean this. Let me clean up, please,' she said, constantly moving around in search for the mop and bucket. She found everything she needed in the dark corner behind the row of file cabinets. The dust resting on the aluminium cabinets gave weight to her judgment of Valentina's cleaning skills.

Ioli picked up the air-conditioning's remote and turned it on. In July, there was no great difference between day temperature and that of late evenings. Only around midnight did you feel a change in temperature and even then, it was still hot. The floorboard creaked as Ioli sat back in the worn-in office chair behind the lone desk. She had one eye on Mrs. Sophia as she cleaned the floor and another on her phone as she flicked through her newly-saved number for Julia, the shoe maker's wife.

'Good evening, Mrs. Julia, this is Lieutenant Ioli Cara. We spoke earlier today...'

'Have you found my husband?' her barely audible voice came through, frustration and despair wrapped around each word.

'I would appreciate if you could come to the station, and please, come with your son.' Ioli thought he would be good support for his mother, yet, also, get a rough idea of him. *'Two birds, one stone, sort of thing.'*

'Oh, God. No, no... Please, tell me...'

'See you, soon,' Ioli replied and pressed the red button on her screen, ending the call. Informing the living about the dead was a necessary evil that came in the job description. It was, for Ioli and most, the hardest part of being a homicide investigator. Definitely, not a conversation she planned to do over the phone.

Just then, the door opened and Alexandro entered, the look on his face puzzling.

'What's wrong with you? Why are you so late?' Ioli

asked, tilting her head to the side and placing it upon her hand.

'Don't ask, just... just watch,' he replied, his palms waving in the air. 'What's going on in there?' he asked, watching Mrs. Sophia mopping the floor.

'Don't ask!'

An exchange of smiles followed, only for the moment to be violently interrupted by the slamming open of the door. A tall man with a thick moustache and a checked-shirt unbuttoned half way, revealing his hairy chest, barged in.

'Come on, city boy. We haven't got all day.'

'Coming, sir,' Alexandro replied and exited, ducking below the man's hand that held the door wide open.

'Well, hello there, pretty lady. I'm Gianni. Valentina's father. Nice to meet you,' he said and bowed his head, leaning his straw cowboy hat forward. His golden chain came out of his thick chest hair and his cross hung down in front of him.

Ioli did not manage to reply as the bulky man turned and left, leaving the door open. Soon, a huge, rusty-in-the-corners ice-cream fridge was being forced through the door, carried by the two men. Valentina followed behind them, giving nervous directions and warning them not to damage the walls.

'Leave it there, by the file cabinets. And, dad, don't forget to plug it in,' she finally said and approached Ioli, her cheeks the color of a red autumn pepper. Witnessing Mrs. Sophia in the holding room, she squatted by Ioli and whispered in her ear. 'The coroner's team will be here first thing in the morning... where were we supposed to leave the body? My father has a kiosk down by the beach and has many old fridges in the back...'

'Say no more. Under the circumstances, it's a good idea.

Now, help me get rid of granny Poppins over there. Mr. Sakis's family is on the way. After I break the shocking news, I'll need you to sit with his wife. I want to find a way to talk to the son, but not in front of his mother,' Ioli replied, in the same whispery manner.

Mrs. Sophia had finished with the cleaning and proceeded with ordering the youth to change clothes. Adonis stood up and with obvious strain and awkward movements he undressed. Mrs. Sophia served him her specialty and placed the hot plate on his bed. 'Eat up, my love.'

'Do you think he's a suspect because Natalie turned him down?' Valentina continued her conversation with Ioli, slightly worried about what her father was talking about to Alexandro.

'If Adonis is innocent, everyone on the island is a suspect. I've seen the most unlikely people do the most awful crimes. It worries me, not only that she turned him down, but because his father -who called in about the true killer- was found murdered hours later. He called from home. Who else could have heard him besides his wife and son?'

Valentina nodded and stood up, her mind thinking over if it was made out for the job. *'Why didn't I think of that?'* she thought as she rushed over to the two men relaxing their strained muscles by the ice-cream fridge housing a corpse-popsicle.

'Single, eh? What are you waiting for? What are you? Twenty-seven? Twenty-eight?'

'Twenty-nine,' Alexandro replied.

'A man needs a good woman in his life...' the man chatted away, while scratching himself every now and then.

Once his jaw, twice his chest and a few times on the back of his head.

'Dad!' Valentina said, using the tone he was so familiar with. She had used it with him ever since her puberty. 'Don't you have to get back home? Mum will be waiting.'

'Hmm, yeah,' he grunted. He placed his hand firmly on Alexandro's shoulder and squeezed it tight. 'Think about it, son.' He, then, smiled to Ioli and added 'Valentina's a fine good cop, you know. Not a very suitable job for a woman as your father surely tells you, but she's really good at it...'

'Dad!'

'I'm gone, I'm gone!' he said and with a steady plod, he exited the building. The uproarious sound from the engine of his truck echoed through the air as Valentina apologized to Ioli.

'No need for that. My father, named Gianni as well, never wanted me to become a cop. Never mind, a homicide detective. Now...' she paused, nodding to the direction of the cell.

'On it,' Valentina said and went over to Mrs. Sophia to inform her of visiting hours, how Adonis should get some sleep and a few more excuses she came up with on the spot.

As Mrs. Sophia kissed her grandson and wished them all a very good night, Ioli's mind travelled to her father. She could not believe it had been nearly a year since he passed away, betrayed by a heart that beat only for his wife and daughter.

Valentina set up her coffee maker and stood there watching as hot, steamy drops fell into the empty glass cylinder below. She knew it took well over seven minutes to prepare, more as she added enough ingredients for five people. She did not ask if anyone wished for it. Valentina wanted to have something better to do than feel Alexandro's eyes on her. She kept her back to him the whole time.

Alexandro decided to get his own *feel* of Adonis.

'Enjoy your chicken?' he asked, as he stood in the doorway of Adonis's cell.

Adonis had left the empty plate on the floor by the door and had climbed back upon the bed. His round blue eyes looked up at Alexandro and as he rocked about anxiously, he reminded Alexandro of the bobbing head dogs that he kept in the back of his white Ford.

Adonis swallowed with a loud noise signalling the journey of his spit downwards. 'Err... Ye... Yes, sir. Grandma's cooking is, is the best.'

'She really loves you, kid. The whole island seems to like you.'

His face lit up like a bulb. His crooked-teeth smile ran from ear to ear. 'Granny is always with me. People here... are... very kind.'

'It's nice to have someone always there for you. Did Natalie like you, too?'

A shadow formed across Adonis's pale face. 'Poor Natalie. If she was less sinful... she would be alive...' His words became difficult to understand and his rocking grew more violent.

'Is that why you used your knife? Because she was a sinner?' Alexandro asked, squatting opposite the blond hair youth with the group of subtle freckles upon his round cheeks.

'No... No...' he yelled the word. 'Never... I like her...'

'And she turned you down?'

'I... I... She was mean... but I did not want... *that* from her, you know... what other boys wanted... I wanted a friend.'

'Who killed her then?' Alexandro inquired, his eyes meeting with the boy's.

Adonis raised his shoulders. 'Beats me!' he replied and giggled.

Just then, a knock on the main door was heard. Alexandro stood up, touched Adonis's hair and wished him a good night's sleep. He closed the door behind him and walked over to Ioli who was rubbing her lower back, having just stood up.

Valentina was ready to call out a 'come in', but as the door immediately flew open after the knock, there was no need.

Mrs. Julia rushed into the room, her red apron with the printed recipe on it was still tied around her waist. Her hair was messy and her eyes moved around like angry dragon-flies in the back garden.

'Where is he?' she shrieked.

'Ma, relax,' the muscular teen behind her, advised. 'Let them talk,' he continued and took a prolonged drag from his shiny, newly-bought, vaping machine.

'Please, he has been gone all day,' she pleaded to Valentina, ignoring her son and the huge cloud of smoke that he released into the room. He yawned, put his hands in his pockets and leaned back, placing his foot upon the no-longer white wall.

Valentina took one look at Ioli who quickly shook her head.

'Sit down with Lieutenant Cara and she will inform you. I'll bring over coffee,' Valentina said and swirled back to her coffee-making station.

Julia placed both her palms upon her sweaty face and pushed back the multiple crinkly brown hairs dangling in front of her eyes. She took a deep breath with her eyes closed and walked calmly towards Ioli and sat down opposite her.

'I am ready,' she announced, and closed her hazel eyes once again.

'Oh, for freakin' sake, ma. This ain't one of ya Mexican soap operas.'

'I'm afraid your husband is dead,' Ioli said in her *trained for such occasions* voice. She placed her hand on Julia's knee, yet kept her eyes on Andreas.

Andreas' vaporizer fell to the ground as he lost his balance. He took a step forward. All blood seemed to have abandoned his face. Ashen, he said: 'shut the front door! You're joking, right? This is some sort of cruel joke. Who would want to hurt my father?'

'Who said someone hurt him?' Ioli replied, her eyes set on the teen.

'I... I...'

The words never came. He fell back and sat against the wall. He placed his head between his knees and remained silent.

'You sure?' Julia finally spoke.

'Yes, Mrs. Julia,' Valentina replied, coming closer to her mother's friend. 'I saw him myself,' she said, hoping no one would ask to see the body. Seeing their loved one, crashed, mutilated and tossed in an old ice-cream fridge was not what they needed at that moment.

'How?'

'We are still investigating the circumstances of how your husband died. We found his body at the bottom of the caldera...'

'Oh, God. Saki...' she cried, her hand covering her mouth. Tears escaped the corners of her eyes where they had grouped together. One by one, they ran freely down her round face.

'Mrs. Julia, your husband called us today and he mentioned that he knew who Natalie's killer was,' Ioli said, retracting her hand and sitting back in the chair. With her six-month old embryo in the way, there was no chance for her to use her usual leaning forward with caring eyes pose that she normally used in such situations.

'Is that why he was... murdered?' she asked, through sobs.

'We don't know for sure that he was murdered or if it's related to Natalie's case. Likely scenarios are just guesses and presumptions until proven facts by the evidence.'

'What else could have happened?'

'He could have fallen. Was he drinking or feeling unwell today?'

'Oh, for fuck's sake. My dad is no dumb villager, lady.'

'Andrea, please,' his mother said and silenced him. 'Saki was fine today. A bit worried, maybe...'

'Did he tell you anything about Natalie's case?'

'No,' she said, shaking her head.

'How about you?'

Andrea raised his head from his knees and stood up. 'I was there with him when he made the call.'

'And?' Alexandro asked, ten seconds into the youth's pause.

'I asked him. All he said to me was that Adonis did not kill her and he rushed out the door, got in his car. I assumed he was coming here.'

Alexandro approached him wearing what he presumed was his good-cop face. 'He said nothing more? Or if he mentioned this to anyone else?'

Andrea just shook his head. His hands kept wiping away

tears. 'I'm going outside. I need a real cigarette,' he said and rushed out the door, leaving it to swing behind him.

'*So much for e-cigs helping you quit,*' Ioli thought. Julia began to try to stand up with shaking hands placed on the arms of the chair. Ioli placed her hand on her shoulder. 'I'll go with him. Stay. Take your time. Drink your coffee.'

The first police captain she had worked with had advised her to use short sentences with victim's families. 'They are in no position to pay attention or think clearly. Keep your questions as short as possible and your sentences shorter,' the Herculean Cretan had said all those years ago and the words had stuck with her ever since.

Valentina came forward with Mrs. Julia's coffee and placed it to her side. She kept her own in her hands and sat down opposite her. She remained silent knowing well that just like any Greek woman, Mrs. Julia would soon start talking about her husband and list all his fine qualities. She wasn't wrong.

Alexandro watched as Valentina walked past him, not offering him a coffee. She had, however, made enough for all. With Ioli outside and Valentina preoccupied with listening to what a good, moral man, Mr. Sakis, was, Alexandro poured himself a cup and stood above the desk, taking slow sips and reading the coroner's report.

The street light on the side road of the station flickered, surrounded by myriads of flying insects of the night. Andrea stood below, leaning back on the dirty green post. He huffed in and released large clouds of smoke. After every other cloud, came a smoke ring.

'I'm guessing a pregnant lady did not come out to enjoy a smoke with me,' he said, watching Ioli walk towards him. He blew his smoke towards the side as she came close.

'Smart boy,' she said, flashing a wide smile.

Andrea's eyes were focused on her white symmetrical teeth. He chuckled and threw his cigarette butt to the ground, next to a homeless soda can. He did not bother stomping it out.

'What's so funny?'

'My dad has a saying about smiles like yours,' he replied.

'And what was that?'

'A smile like that opens a lot of doors, but opens even more wallets,' he said, deepening his voice, apparently mimicking his old man. 'I... I can't believe he's gone,' he continued, holding back sobs. He crossed the road and sat down on a neglected wooden bench. Ioli followed and joined him.

'My father passed away last year. I, too, could not believe it. It took a while to accept it. I think, lonely children like us are even more attached to our parents. You know? It's always the three of us and all their attention is on us.'

'Was he murdered?'

'No, heart attack...'

'Then, you have no idea of the anger I am feeling, right now. Just because of that stupid slut, my father is dead. He was such a lawful kind of guy. The Christian type to always do good. Look where that got him. He just had to meddle. Got himself stuck in all this shit.'

Andrea spoke with heavy breathing; his hands clenched together in fists.

'Were you friends with Adonis?'

'Not really. We all played with him during primary school. I remember his first day, here in Folegandros. Our second grade teacher told us a new boy was coming to our school. She gave a huge speech about how he has special needs and had just lost his mother, so we all played with him. But, as we grew older and he remained a child, we all kind of lost touch,' he said and after a pause added, 'even without my dad saying so, there is no way that Adonis would have killed that whore.'

'I'm guessing you weren't a big fan of Natalie's.'

'I know she's dead and all, and we aren't supposed to talk bad about the dead, but she was one of a kind. The bad kind. Slept around with everyone in school.'

Ioli gazed up at the night sky, filled with shiny stars as far as the eye could focus. She acted casually as she threw the question to which she already knew the answer.

'You, too?'

Andrea sat up straight. For the first time in the last half an hour, his father left his mind. Now, there was a beautiful woman sitting next to him, asking about his sex life. The teen's cheeks started to rose up slightly.

'Erm, no. I had a girlfriend for most of the year.'

'Really? Because I saw in the case file that you were her prom date. Bet you were over the moon to have the most popular girl in school on your arm.'

Andrea played around with his fingers and looked away. 'Well, you know. It was like, I was sure to score. I had just broken up with the girl I told you I was with...' he paused, unsure on how to proceed.

'But, I thought you said you never slept with her?' Ioli asked, continuing her clueless act.

'Yeah, we got into a silly fight and went our separate ways for the night. Turned out for the best. I'm back with my girl,' he said and Ioli caught a glimpse of a faint smile.

'A fight?'

Andrea turned towards Ioli, his facial characteristics turning hard. 'I know you're investigating her death, but why do you care about the stupid dance and this ancient history shit? Anyway, you should be spending your time finding the bastard who killed my father,' he said, raising his voice.

Ioli remained calm, exhaling deeply. 'Andrea, if your father's death is connected to Natalie's, then everything I found out is helping to catch the bastard. What might be remembered in your mind as a silly fight, could hold evidence for me. Anything you know about Natalie could help.'

His eyes narrowed. He leaned forward and cracked his fingers. He took his time and Ioli let him. Finally, he stood up, walked around for a minute and came back to her. 'You didn't hear this from me,' he said and sat back down beside her.

'I would never reveal a source.'

'We fought because she told me she only came with me because a popular girl like her could not be seen at our graduation party alone. She said she had a boyfriend and it was serious. No *high school dating shit* as she put it. She would not say who he was. Only that he was too grown up for a kiddie dance. I called her a whore and I spent the rest of the night with my mates. However, the next day I found out who her mystery lover was. I could not leave it; you know? Part of me thought she was lying and had just played a cruel joke on me.'

He pulled out his wrinkled packet of cigarettes. He looked down at Ioli's tummy and slid away from her to the end of the bench. The lighter's flame shone on his acne-riddled face as the end of the cigarette came to life. He blew the smoke in the opposite direction of Ioli.

Ioli smiled and asked, 'how did you find out?'

'I knew a secret I could use. Natalie did not have any girl friends. She never got along with girls. Boys were always potential lovers or creeps she would not spit on if they were on fire. She only had one true friend. Christopher.'

'Who's Christopher?' Ioli asked, her mind wondering how come this was the first time she was hearing the name. Neither her family nor school *friends* mentioned him.

'A classmate of ours. The big secret is that Christopher is gay,' he said, pausing to stare at Ioli's expression. 'Not a big deal in the city, but here in a town of five hundred, it's something that could ruin you and your family. Christopher is handsome, the Calvin Klein model kind of handsome. Natalie probably hit on him on the first chance she caught him alone. Obviously, he never slept with her and since then, they became best friends. You see, Christopher became the male version of Natalie. Through Facebook and God knows what other social media, Christopher met men. Men who came for holidays here and Christopher would hook up with them at their hotel rooms. He kept it all very hush-hush, not only out of fear from gossip, but because he was only sixteen when it all started.'

Every now and then, he paused and took long drags, blowing out clouds of smoke that quickly evaporated in the night breeze that ran freely through the dark narrow streets.

'You seem to know a lot about Christopher. And why would he confide to you about Natalie's secret lover?'

His cigarette dropped to the cold grey pavement. He stepped on the butt as it tried to run away, carried by the cool air. He slid back next to Ioli. His eyes scanning the area, making sure they were alone.

'Christopher and I were good mates. Friends since Miss Stella sat us together in fifth grade. When we were fifteen, Christopher came on to me. He kissed me and groped me. That was pretty much the end of our close friendship, yet we still talked. I knew how close he was with Nat. So, the day after the party I paid him a visit demanding to know who Natalie was seeing. His lips were sealed until I threatened to tell his dad about him bending over to every Tom, Dick and Harry. He warned me as I am about to warn you. Be careful. He is more powerful than you can imagine,' he whispered and paused.

'Who was she seeing?' Ioli asked, feeling time flying by as the boy poured out his heart.

'The mayor,' he replied, his eyes opening wide.

'I knew it! That sleazy...'

'Shh, keep your voice down. You don't get it. He is like the mafia. He has his hands on everything on the island and nearby islands. Black money. Dad used to say his lawyer wife helps him cover the trails. No one speaks out of fear. They only vote for him because they owe him money. Natalie told Christopher that the mayor was going to break up with his wife for her after the election. Bullshit, if you ask me. You see, he can't afford to lose the election because he uses the town hall books to cover his dirty work or so, dad used to say. Dad fixed the town hall's coffee-lady's shoes. He used to laugh about having inside intel.'

'And what dirty work is this?'

'I have no idea. But, I know one thing. No way is he letting Helen win the election. She is mad for going up against him. She is the first to ever oppose him. Mama says she must have something against him as she is still alive.'

'*Maybe she knew about Natalie*,' Ioli thought, nodding her head.

Chapter Thirteen

ON BOARD

I stood outside the thick door of the ship Captain's office. Emphasis on the thick part as I could hear nothing from the ongoing conversation inside. The engine clanks and loud waves splashing, echoing from outside, did not help either. They were powerful enough to cover the teacher's cries as Nick and Katerina discussed with the Captain the 'messy situation below'.

I wore my brown trousers and a white shirt on top, both newly-bought by Tracy. No one would take a beach-wearing, middle age man with no badge, seriously. Technically, I had no authority. I was on medical leave until further notice. Either of cure or of death.

The teacher came out first; the door closed abruptly behind her. Nick Pavlou slammed it closed while wiping his sweaty red forehead. His perfect black hair having surrendered to a massive amount of hair gel, did not move an inch from the air wave he created.

'Excuse me,' I said, approaching the school teacher, who

looked paler that a white sheet in a detergent commercial. 'Mrs. Anne, is it?'

She turned towards the direction of my voice and wiped her nose with her magnolia handkerchief, the one with the sewed-in message of love; a present from students past. 'Oh, you're the gentleman from next door. You mentioned you work for the police?'

'Captain Costa Papacosta,' I said, extending my right hand. Her trembling hand was cold compared to the hot surroundings.

'How are the... authorities, handling things?' I asked, trying to sound casual, just a caring passenger and did my best to not mock the word authorities.

'Oh, the security man said to not discuss anything with anyone.'

'I'm sure he did.'

'Can I ask you a rather sensitive question, Mrs. Anne? Have you noticed any form of bullying among your pupils?'

She took a step back, her right hand journeyed up, scratched her neck and played with her silver necklace that held the diamond letters of her name. A present too expensive to be from a student, more likely from her other half.

'That is a deep discussion, Captain. One I would not mind having with you, if not my fear that you are implying another pupil did this to hapless Holly.'

'I never imply anything, ma'am. I check facts. I found a poem in her room about bullying. Could mean nothing,' I replied and took out my phone. 'Did you teach Holly? Is this her handwriting?'

Mrs. Anne searched for her reading glasses in her shirts' top pocket, then patted her black shorts' pockets. 'Where are my darn glasses when I need them?'

My eyes were focused on the round-lensed glasses

comfortably nested in her cauliflower, auburn-turning-white hair. I coughed and pointed with my bushy eyebrows. Actually, since chemotherapy, they had thinned out. The only loss of hair on my body, I can list on the positive side.

'Silly me,' she said, relocating them to her eyes. 'Yep, that's definitely Holly's. It took quite a few stern recommendations for her to give up decorating her capital *I*s. She complained that she had already given up putting smiley faces in the round letters and even hearts on her lower case *I*s. Holly was an artist, not one for the books,' she said, and melancholia shadowed her face.

Just then, the Captain's door opened. Anne smiled at me and walked off at a fast pace. Talking about bullying, Nick Pavlou had frightened the teacher into not talking to anyone or informing the girl's family yet. As if teenagers with phones glued to their hands had not already informed the entire world through social media. Nick's main mission was to prevent the name of the company from being stained.

The group of three exited the room together. All silenced as they noticed me standing in the hallway, looking toward their direction. I walked up to them and introduced myself to the ship's Captain.

A heavily-built man, around my age, with large facial features, he firmly shook my hand and said 'ah, yes. The police captain Nick told me about. There is no need to worry, sir. We are investigating the situation and...'

'Oh, but I do worry. You see, sir, I solve crimes for a living. I have been on homicide cases for as long as you have been on ships. I am sure, Nick is good as a security guy, but he is in over his head, here.'

Nick took a step forward and his mouth opened, ready to shout. Yet, his girlfriend's hand upon his chest prevented any words from exiting into the world.

'There is no body,' the Captain said. 'I cannot have a police man searching around the ship, interrogating guests that have paid good money to relax...'

'A girl could be dead,' Mrs. Anne said, raising her voice. She had remained hidden behind the corner. She could not believe these people's priorities. 'And, if you are so worried about the rest of the guests, did you ever stop to think that you may have a killer on board?'

The Captain stood before me, puzzled and lost for words.

'What do you believe is our best course of action?' he finally raised his troubled head and asked.

'Let me handle the case and keep this guy out of my way.'

'What a jerk! But, what can you expect from a cop?' Nick said and scoffed.

I paid no attention to macho, muscle-built, single-cell brained men in the past and I did not plan to start on a sunny day like today. I kept my eyes on the Captain.

'Sir, I believe the other kids know or hold information vital to the girl's whereabouts. I said whereabouts, Mrs Anne, as I suspect the girl could very well still be alive. The scene is too staged to be an assault and murder scene,' I said, and Mrs. Anne's face lit up and she placed her cold hands on my arm.

'Captain, the vase on the bedside table was dropped on the floor by the door. It was not thrown. It did not smash all over the place. The jewelry box was perfectly placed by the pool of blood with a note hinting to bullying. Talking about the blood, there is way too much blood and it is all concentrated in the middle of the carpet. If there was a body, there would be blood spatter or marks where the body was dragged or lifted out of the cabin. Sir, Mrs. Anne, I know my job. Let me speak to the kids, let me go through their rooms. I can solve this.'

Nick spoke first, leaving me in question if I had managed to convince the teacher and the captain of granting me access. 'You believe the blood was just dumped there? And, how would a kid find so much blood anyway?'

'I *guess, I can't avoid talking to you,*' I thought and turned to his direction.

'Yes, I do. And, I don't think it is human blood. That is where I need your help, doc. We have to test it, to be sure. It would offer us all great relief.'

The doctor slightly licked her lips before she spoke. 'We could call Syros hospital to have some anti-human serum ready for me and as soon as we dock, I could take a sample of our blood and have it tested. If it coagulates it is human.'

'Let's hope it doesn't then. And, to answer your other question Nick. It is easy to obtain pig's blood and bring it in bottles on board. No one weighs the suitcases. That is the first thing I want to check. Whose luggage is half-empty. And, look for the bottles used. I will start with Holly's if that is okay with you,' I said, my eyes going back and forth from the teacher to the captain.

'My pupils are sixteen and seventeen. I don't have the authority to let you question them without their parents knowing.'

'You sound like you know what you're doing, sir, and you have my permission to access the cabins,' the captain said. 'But, if I can offer a piece of advice. Let's keep this a secret from the students. Mrs. Anne can gather her pupils in the cinema room while you search.'

'That sounds illegal,' Mrs. Anne commented, turning in my direction.

'She's got a point. We don't only want to solve this case,

but if a crime was committed, we need our evidence to stand in court,' I said.

'Actually, by the Greek sea regulations, the ship's Captain can search all places on board if he believes it's in the ship's best interest or if he/she suspects illegal activity. I will be with Captain Papacosta at all times and I will be the one to retrieve any evidence. You, Mrs. Anne will be present as the kids' guardian at the moment.'

'And, as for the kids, I will speak to them in terms of a friendly chat,' I added.

Our smiles showed our agreement. The doctor smiled along with us, glad of the outcome. Nick had no such reason; he remained with a stiff face, unhappy with the 'tourist-cop' interfering with what he considered to be his 'department'.

'Oh, and one last question?' I asked the ship-governing Captain.

'Hmm?' he replied, lost in thought.

'I haven't noticed any security cameras in the halls. You have one outside your door. Where else are there cameras?'

'Only in a few areas. None in the halls. A couple on deck, but they point to the bar register. We set them up with employees in mind, not guests. No one wants to be filmed while on holiday.'

'Still, could you have someone check the footage during the last few hours? You never know. We might have a glimpse of the missing girl.'

A Greek man of another generation, he spoke few words. He nodded in agreement and walked off to find the ship's tech.

Chapter Fourteen

The clicking of the door closing behind her sounded divine.

'*Finally alone,*' Ioli thought, standing in the middle of her hotel room with the beautiful fitted carpet and the wooden out-dated furniture.

She undressed slowly, leaving only her black underwear on. She sat on the corner of the bed, first rubbing her strained neck and then, her aching feet. The case played through her mind. Then, she started thinking of the long planned day ahead tomorrow. From the coroner's team arriving for the body, to the signed warrants to search Adonis's and the mayor's houses for Natalie's head.

'*If Adoni had the head, the grandma would have mentioned it or hid it by now... I have to interview more people, if Mr. Sakis saw the crime, maybe someone else did too... Why didn't he come forward straight away? Afraid of the mayor? ... and, what dirty business is he into? ... I must call HQ to have someone investigate his so-called business dealings...*'

The plethora of thoughts running freely in her head helped her headache to metamorphosize into a raging migraine. Ioli took two Remedol pills, called HQ and informed Captain Drako about the possibility of illegal activities by the mayor of Folegandros.

'Send me the files and I'll look into it. If there is something to it, I'll send an officer to the island,' he said, his stern voice bringing a smile to Ioli's tired face. None of the department's secretaries lasted long with him; his steely manners terrified them when deadlines or standards were not met. He insisted that deep down he was a 'good guy'. 'Deeper than an oil drill can go,' his last secretary had said as she requested a change of station.

As he spoke, Ioli heard a faint beep and saw the envelope sign flickering on her cell. A message from the coroner. As soon as she thanked Captain Drako and said goodbye, she lowered her phone and read the coroner's note.

'The girl was pregnant. Three to four weeks into her pregnancy,' she read and then closed her eyes. 'Oh, God, what is this case I've gotten myself into to?' she wondered and wiped the corners of her sore eyes.

Her next action was to take a long cold bath. She stood under the shower head for as long as her feet allowed her to. With a blank mind, she let the water fall to her black hair and travel down her body, offering relief to her heated skin pores. She dried herself quickly and clumsily, and walked over to the bed while still drying her soaking wet hair.

'Oh, come on, universe! Shit,' she said, rolling her eyes. Her phone lay alone in the middle of the white bed sheet. It flashed Mark's face, signalling his missed call. With the blue hotel towel wrapped around her, she picked up her phone, swearing more as she read that he had called her three times.

'Doesn't call me all evening and night, and as soon as I

get in the shower...' she ranted, blowing away the wet hair swinging in front of her eyes.

She listened to the echoing beeps as she waited for Mark to answer.

'At last!'

'Hey, Babe. I was in the shower,' Ioli said in the sweetest tone she could manage at such an hour.

'You know I worry when you don't pick up. Especially when you're on a case. Take it with you in the bathroom,' he said and Ioli could picture him pacing up and down in their two-bedroom apartment.

'I just really needed a shower. It's been a long day...'

'I hope you're taking care of yourself,' he interrupted her.

'I'm not stupid, Mark. I would not risk our baby,' Ioli said and sat down on the bed, her eyes watching a moth flying around the strong-light bulb dangling from the ceiling.

'Well, you did take this case.'

'Hit me when I'm down why don't you? You know what? Screw you, Mark and thanks for the support.'

She lowered her hand, listening to his reply fading, and ended the call. Her screen went dark and she covered her mouth, releasing a muted scream. Her phone came back to life, vibrating besides her. Mark's smiling face and his deep dimples that she loved, appeared on the screen. She hesitated for a few seconds and finally picked up.

'What?'

'You could not have guessed that the case would require you to stay. Sorry. But, when you get back, you're taking time off and not going back after your maternity leave ends.'

'I hate your *buts* after you say something right. I'll leave when I want to leave. I don't intervene in your work, doctor.'

'That's different. You risk your life daily and at the moment, you are carrying another life with you. Our son. I think I get a say in that. Besides, you will be back to work in no time. I don't understand why...'

'Lieutenant promotions are next month. I'm sure, I will be promoted from B to Lieutenant A. I don't want to give anyone any excuses. There are only going to be three openings.'

'And then? Dedicated your life to work, to become a Captain? And then? Baby, we are starting a family. When did you turn so career-oriented?'

'Since I've been doing this for fourteen years and I deserve it. I hate you implying that I will take time away from my family. My family will be my number one priority. But, my job is my job. I love it and I deserve this. Anyway, I can't do this right now. I'm tired. All's good. Stop worrying. Talk tomorrow,' she said in a rush, closed the phone and fell back on the uncomfortable pillow.

Tears formed in the corners of her eyes. 'Fucking hormones,' she said, wiping them away and turning off the light.

Chapter Fifteen

Father Kallinikos awoke before the sun.

His inner clock worked better than a Swiss Breitling. Under the sound of his wife's blithely snoring and in total darkness thanks to his light-hating other half's blackout blinds, he wore his black rasa, vestment and placed his kali-mavkion on his going-bald head. He sneaked out the room, closing the door silently behind him. None of his six kids heard him and that, for Father Kallinikos, was truly a bless-ing. The last thing he needed at such an hour were requests for water or worse, to come and play. He entered his humble kitchen, grabbed two slices of Greek homemade bread, two juicy peaches, a tin of chicken-flavored dog food and a bottle of iced water. He, then, thanked God for another day on Earth and exited the side door, whistling happily to the tune of Byzantine hymns. His faithful Labrador sprang up and ran to him, maniacally jumping around him and licking his fingers.

'Good morning, Maximus. Who's a good boy? Who's a

good boy, eh? Where's your lead? Go get your lead. Quickly.'

The white Labrador with the fair haired back and the black sock on his front left leg, ran into his wooden home and dashed out with his walking rope in his drooling mouth.

By the time the pair of friends exited the freshly-painted, white wooden fence, the first sun rays had sneaked through the gaps between houses and illuminated the dark paved road. Father Kallinikos stopped his stroll, scratched his thick, long, black beard and took a moment to gaze into the rising sun. He breathed in the fresh morning air that travelled carrying the scent of the Mediterranean and again, thanked the Lord for another day. He turned his head towards the hill that rose beside the town. A long, snakelike, dirt road climbed the dried-up mountainous region, ending outside the church of the Virgin Mary. Panagia, as she is referred to by the Greeks. Built to overlook the good citizens of Chora, it was mostly used for special occasions, weddings and christenings. The three churches in town were used for Sunday mass. The Cycladic church had breath-taking unobstructed views of the cliff, the town and the Aegean Sea. It was no surprise that it had turned into a must-see location for visitors to the small island. This fact was the main reason that Father Kallinikos had locked the church door for the last six years or so. The church council did not trust tourists to refrain from damaging or stealing the sacred building and its priceless historical possessions. Many elderly women on the committee also commented on the lack of clothing noticed on the 'females from abroad'.

Father Kallinikos took his time to enjoy the scenic route. He had all the time in the world or so he wished to believe. The church council meeting was at nine and he wanted to prepare his office. He was also looking forward to an hour of praying without being interrupted by one of his offspring.

Forty-five minutes later, he pulled out his set of keys from his deep pocket and approached the gargantuan front door. With the strength of his youthful age of thirty-two, he pushed the heavy door, did the sign of the cross and entered the capacious church. The incense tickled his nose as it lingered in the confined air.

'Stay!' he ordered Maximus, and entered the side room which served as his office. Soon, he reappeared with a metal bowl filled with dog food in his right hand. He laid the food in front of the canine, expecting him to devour his breakfast as usual. The dog did not move a muscle.

'What's wrong, boy?' he asked, noticing the dog's focused gaze towards the altar. There was nothing Father Kallinikos could see. He began to walk towards the iconostasis when Maximus started to bark frantically. Kallinikos stopped and stared at his friend. He had never acted this way before and having faith in his canine senses, he did something he hoped the ladies of the church committee would never find out; he called Maximus into the church. The dog took hesitant steps as he entered the once forbidden grounds. He turned to check with his master.

'Go on, boy. What's wrong?'

Maximus ran along the red carpet and entered the sanctuary, howling wolf-like cries.

'God forgive me,' Kallinikos said, witnessing the animal entering the Holy space. Alarmed by his dog's peculiar behavior, he once again did the sign of the cross and quickly ran towards Maximus. The dog exited the sanctuary and came to his side.

'Oh, dear Lord,' he gasped. The dog's mouth and nose were red. 'Is that blood?' he asked and slowly took heavy steps towards the altar behind the icons. Lost for words, he fell to his knees. Natalie's sawed-off head lay in the middle of the table, both her eyes severely stabbed; rigor-mortis having left her mouth eternally opened in shock. The flies walking along her tongue and the bloody skin tissue that was once attached to the rest of her body would from now on remain engraved in Father Kallinikos' mind. Not a fan of anything modern, he did not own a cell phone. He had to find the strength to run back to his office to call the police from the landline. Panting and sweating, he picked up the receiver and realizing that the line was dead, Father Kallinikos did something he had never done before in church.

'Shit!' he cursed.

Meanwhile, in town, Ioli had also risen before the sun. She did not want her warrants to go to waste or give the Mayor any chance to destroy evidence. She rallied Alexandro and Valentina at the station at seven o'clock sharp.

As the station's door opened, Ioli rushed to the fax machine, while Valentina ran to the coffee maker. Alexandro left the door opened and proceeded to open the two windows, letting the last cool air of the day float into the room. Soon, the heat would be verging on unbearable. He then picked up Andrea's broken e-cigarette from the floor.

'I have considered taking up vaping. You know, they have more flavors than freaking ice-creams. Coconut, cookie and cream, all fruit. A mate of mine even smokes beer-flavored vape,' he said as he placed it on the desk, his eyes focused on Valentina. 'It surely beats plain old bitter tobacco smoke, right?'

'I believe our vices should leave a bitter taste in our

mouths. The damage is the main part of smoking and drinking, is it not?' Valentina replied, her eyes focused on her coffee-making task.

'Not here yet,' Ioli said having checked the fax machine, and sat back into the office chair behind her, wheeling back a foot or two. 'Where are those croissants you picked up from the kiosk?' she asked Alexandro, who stood by the doorway, ready to enjoy his second cigarette of the day.

'Oh, yeah,' he said, and dashed outside to bring the forgotten bag from the car.

Soon, all three were enjoying a strong Greek coffee accompanied with a chocolate croissant. Their breakfast in silence was interrupted by the screeching sound of the fax machine coming to life.

'At last,' Ioli mumbled, her mouth full with her third croissant. She leaped out of her chair and stood above the exiting pieces of paper.

'Valentina, you will go to Mrs. Sophia's house. Alone. Be as thorough as you can. This time, look everywhere. In wardrobes, the kitchen, closets, garden shed, everywhere. Adonis is still our main suspect. Alexandro and I, will take on the much larger Mayor's house. We need to find evidence of his relationship with Natalie, but also...' she said and paused to swallow the last piece of chocolate filling. She, then, turned to Alexandro '... I will need you, to check his office computer and files while I distract him. Our case is Natalie and Mr. Sakis, of course, however, if we find anything to help the investigation behind his dodgy business that would be a great help.

Inside his cell, Adonis stood wide awake, listening in. He did not understand much and was intrigued by the new word *warrant*. His attention was drawn away from the conversation as a crawling cockroach ran by his bare foot.

'Eww,' Adonis said in disgust, his gaze following the insect racing around the room in circles before finally bee lining towards the toilet in the corner.

Adonis chuckled. 'Oh, yeah. I didn't pee when I got up.'

He looked down at his bulge in his Winnie the Poor underwear and giggled again. 'Morning erections are normal, says Granny,' he spoke to himself in a whispery manner. 'Good... blood something,' he continued as he lowered his boxer shorts to the floor, and took his penis in his hand. 'Yeah... very normal... try peeing with it, nan!' he said as he tried to pee in the toilet. His laughter was heard outside.

'Guess he is up. I'll take him some juice and something to eat before heading to Mrs. Sophia's house,' Valentina said.

'Meet us at the Mayor's house when you're done,' Ioli commented and with a nod to Alexandro, walked out the door, warrant in hand.

'See you later,' Alexandro said with a wide smile to Valentina. 'Your coffee was great.'

'Thanks,' she said and turned away, presumably to prepare breakfast for their prisoner.

Ioli and Alexandro were going to take the lone police vehicle. Valentina had proposed it, stating that the mayor's house was further in distance, however, Alexandro knew she had given her car because of Ioli's pregnancy.

'*She knew such a statement would provoke the wrath of the mainland Lieutenant. She has a good heart, that one,*' Alexandro thought as he started the engine. A man who enjoyed being called a *player* from those close to him and with quite a few notches on his headboard, he could not truly understand his fascination with the girl from Folegandros. His mama had warned him about these feelings.

'Be careful. Going from girl to girl, you are going to miss the right one,' his father had commented, after he announced that he had broken up with his latest girlfriend.

'Don't worry, dear,' his mother had said. 'When he meets the right one, his heart will turn and twist, and he will be helpless at her feet,' she continued, throwing a wink at her son.

Ioli's voice cut his daydreaming about the past.

'You know; I never did ask you. What made you become a cop?'

Alexandro's reason fell into Ioli's category of a *good story*.

'I must have been seven or eight at the time. I went with my mother to the supermarket and as a spoiled child, I got to throw into the trolley a bunch of chocolates and sweets. I guess that is what shocked me most with the little girl crying in the aisle. All she wanted was a packet of biscuits. Her father spoke so viciously towards her. He spat as he yelled no. 'It's just biscuits, daddy', she said and he slapped her so hard, the poor girl banged against the hard shelves and split her lip. 'See what you get, when you're naughty', he said and did nothing to help her get up. I was shocked to see that no one did anything. No one went to help, no one spoke. I felt that the girl was helpless, so I rushed to her side and picked her up,' Alexandro said and then smiled. 'I gave that mean old bastard such a dirty look,' he continued. 'What you looking at?' Alexandro mimicked the man's voice. 'A bully,' I replied. 'A malaka that hits kids. You should be arrested!' I yelled. I think he would have smacked me, too, if my mother had not run over and apologized. 'Don't ever hurt her again', I continued yelling as my mother pulled me away. The girl's smile was the best thing I took home with me that day. I was grounded for a week, but it was worth it. Since then, I set my mind on protecting the innocent. Okay, back then, I had pictured it more along the lines of a vigilante, like Bruce Wayne. As I was a couple of billion short of becoming Batman, I settled on being a cop,' he said, finishing his story with a gloating grin.

'Wow, that's a wicked story,' Ioli commented.

Alexandro remained silent for the rest of the drive, reliving the supermarket moment in his mind.

Alexandro's preoccupation with his thoughts came to an end as he turned uphill and entered the road with the rows of palm trees. The grand manor welcomed them with a tall locked gate.

'Expected,' Ioli said, and stepped out of the running vehicle. She approached the silver-painted gate and pressed the intercom button built into the brick wall. No reply came. Ioli stared into the two cameras towering her from the columns by the side of the gates. She wondered if the mayor was looking at her at that very moment and not opening the fancy gate. She pressed the button again.

'Yes, yes. Who is it? Stop ringing, please,' a woman's voice came through the speaker, loud and clear and in broken English.

'This is Lieutenant Ioli Cara,' she introduced herself, showing her badge into the camera. 'Police,' she added.

'Come back later, Madame. Boss asleep now.'

'This is the police. I don't care who's asleep, you open this gate right now or I will be forced to shoot it open and then arrest you for obstruction of justice!'

Inside, Rashmi Singhe bit her bottom lip. Her eyes were focused on the lady waving her police badge. Leaving Sri Lanka two years ago at the tender age of eighteen, the anxiety of what she would find in Greece was high. She had heard from compatriots of hers about living in isolated villages having to take care of seniors, including their baths and toilet visits, having to take care of spoiled little rich brats that bullied and ordered them around, and she had even heard of a few cases of abuse and sexual harassment. Much to her delight, she arrived at the charming and quaint island of Folegandros, to work at the most luxurious house she had ever laid eyes upon. She had her own room, bath and kitchen. Nothing like sharing a room with her three sisters back in Dambulla. Her joy continued when she realized there were no kids or seniors in the house. 'A normal family of three,' she had thought at the time. But time went by and Rashmi, though enjoying *the good life*, realized the family that employed her, was far from normal. She was closer to becoming an astronaut than this family was to being normal. She lived with three living clichés or at least that was what her reality TV shows had taught her. The teenager hated her parents, ignored them all day with her headphones glued into her ears, smoked weed in her room and climbed out her window at nights. The wife spent money like there was no tomorrow, had no idea where the kitchen was in her house and slept with the gardener, the pool boy and any other boy with a six-pack that complimented her. The husband was no better when it came to respecting his wedding vows. He, also, had a thing for sleeping with people half his age. 'His latest mistress could not be older than his own daughter,' she had gossiped with her mother over the phone after seeing Natalie leave the master bedroom. The not normal part came from the boss' visitors. Visitors that always came around midnight. Characters you wished you never bumped into in a dark alley. They either came with wrapped-up packages and left with briefcases filled with cash or came with cases and left with packages. Rashmi knew well that no legal business took place at such hours, so having a police officer at the gates came to no surprise. The dilemma, though, did. She wasn't expecting to get caught in the middle of it all. Should she first awake her boss, leave the police waiting and risk being arrested? Or should she open the gate, cooperate with police and then wake her boss?

'Excuse me?' Ioli's angry voice made her jump.

Rashmi wiped away her forehead's cold sweat and chose to open the gates. As she watched the police officer return to her car and drive up the gravelled road that led up to the majestic fountain of Apollo, outside the house's entrance, Rashmi felt her blood run thicker in her veins. She dashed upstairs in a hurry to wake the mayor. She slid on the shiny marble stairs and fell forward. Reflexes kicked in and her hands saved her face from hitting the hard ground, only inches away. She stood up in a hurry and continued her run to the master bedroom's door.

'Oh, I hope he doesn't have some underage girl in there with him,' she whispered to herself in Sinhalese. She knocked on the door, violently, unlike her discreet maid's knocking. It took a while before a grunt from inside the room was heard. She opened the carved pine-wood door only a few inches and with her eyes turned the other way, she took two reluctant steps inside. The boss had the habit of sleeping in the nude on top of the sheets. She learned that information the hard way; a lesson of *show and don't tell* of sorts.

'What the hell, Rashmi? It's fucking night time still!'

'The police are at the door, ordering me to let them in,' she said; her throat closing up with every other word.

'Tall pregnant lady with straight black hair?' he inquired, sitting up and searching for his Versace boxer shorts.

'That's the one, sir. And, another younger man.'

'Don't worry, Rashmi. She is less dangerous than my wife's Chihuahua. Let them in and see them to the lounge. Tell them, I am dressing and will be with them shortly.'

'*Fucking more questions about Natalie,*' he thought and walked over to his en-suite to relieve his whiskey-filled bladder.

Outside, Ioli and Alexandro stood side by side in front of the resplendent front door.

'All good with the baby? How are you coping? If you don't mind me asking.'

'I'm fine. Baby has been good to me, letting me do my job,' Ioli replied, instinctively placing her hand upon her tummy.

'Why didn't you mention the warrant?' Alexandro asked, staring down at his black boots. Nothing he hated more than dirt on his shoes.

'Because he would stall and never open the door until he had hidden anything he wished to hide. He thinks I am here to grill him about Natalie.'

Alexandro nodded in agreement. Ioli thought it was funny how he posed when waiting for a door to open. He stood up straight, broadened his shoulders and his serious-looking face was more still than a Madame Tussaud's waxwork. Ioli called it his 'bodyguard pose'. Maybe it was a way to deal with his height. Ioli was taller than him, even now in her flats.

The opening of the door cut into her thoughts. Rashmi smiled nervously in front of them.

'This way, this way,' she said with her hand extended. 'Please come through. Mayor Stamos is in his bedroom getting dressed and will be with you shortly...'

Ioli walked past her, papers in hand. 'What's your name?'

'Rashmi, Madame...'

'I'm no Madame, thank you very much. Rashmi, this here is a warrant. We are going to search the house, the entire house. You are going to stay put; over there on those fine looking sofas and you will be joined by your boss shortly. Who else is in the building?'

Rashmi took a step back. 'Erm, just Miss Anna.'

'And where is she?' Alexandro asked as he wandered from them, his eyes wide open in awe as he studied the marble staircase that stood like a twister in the middle of the grand vast room.

'Up... Upstairs, in her bedroom,' the young girl replied, taking more steps back and having finally reached the sofa, she sat down. She placed her hands between her legs and bit her lips. Her heartbeats doubled and she closed her eyes, praying to Buddha for his guidance, by repeating her favorite mantra.

Ioli smiled at her. 'You have nothing to worry about. Just stay there,' Ioli advised and started to ascend the long winding flight of stairs. 'Search around the ground floor. I will send them down and then search upstairs,' she said, turning to Alexandro, who had begun to follow her to the upstairs floor.

'Sure,' he said and turned around. He hopped off the last step, looked left and right and walked off towards the dining area. Ioli paused to stare at him. One thing she liked about him was the *no long discussions* part. He was not one to judge her or disagree with something she said or propose a new way of action.

Twenty steps later, Ioli found herself upon a luxurious soft Persian carpet. In both directions, long corridors ran along towards large oval windows. Bright light came through them, shining on the white walls and the golden frames of Renaissance artwork. The door to her left had a pink frame hanging on it. ANNA, it read. Ioli approached and knocked firmly on the door. No reply. She placed her hand on the door knob and pushed the door open. She did not need to go close to the bed to notice that the curves below the peach-colored sheets did not belong to a person, but to a row of pillows.

'What the hell?' Orestis Stamos' morning voice boomed from down the corridor. 'What the hell are you doing up here? Now, this is police harassment. You have no right...' he shouted as he took quick heavy steps towards her. His rant came to an abrupt end when Ioli held out the warrant, stopping only inches from his face.

'I told you, you would see me again, and soon.'

'You bitch! You got a warrant on me? On what grounds? I'm calling my wife immediately. This can't be right,' he sputtered as he reached for his Blackberry.

'One.'

'One what?' he yelled, his fingers trembling as he flicked through his phone.

'One curse word that I am so kind to let slide. You curse at me again and I will arrest you for offending an officer of the law. And you are not really going to call your wife, are you? You really want her to find out about Natalie? Besides, a warrant is a warrant. No lawyer can save you.'

Oresti Stamos looked at the strong-willed woman opposite him. For the first time in his life, he felt that he was not in full control of a situation. He took his time, before speaking.

'Okay, okay,' he said, extending his palms. 'You want evidence that Natalie was here? No need. I will sign a statement that I was indeed having a sexual affair with the girl. But I did not kill her. She left here around midnight all fine and happy. I would never hurt her. I begged her to stay. She was such a sweet young girl. I had no reason to kill her. I... I loved her.'

'You can give me that statement, Mayor. But there is no way in hell that I am not searching your house,' she replied and walked past him. She stood at the head of the stairwell. 'Now, if you may, sir? Please go sit by your maid or I will arrest you for obstruction of justice.' The last sentence was wrapped around by a strong official tone.

Ioli could not decide what to name the color of red that mayor's face took on, nor what to compare it to. Tomato, pepper, beet, lobster. All of them ran through her mind.

'Let me at least wake my daughter. I don't need you scaring the living daylights out of her...'

'There's much going on in this house that is kept secret. Your daughter probably stayed out all night. Those are pillows under her sheets. She should be back shortly, I presume. What time does she believe you wake up?'

The mayor looked lost for words. 'Ten... ish,' he mumbled as he stormed by her defeated, his shoulders lowered.

'By the way, Natalie was pregnant. One month into her pregnancy. Would you like to be informed if it was yours? It's a simple DNA test.'

Stamos froze on the spot. Ioli could not see his face. He just stood still for a whole minute and then continued his descent, without saying a word. Ioli looked on as he went and sat down on the corner of the white sofa. He and Rashmi did not exchange words. She knew well to not talk unless spoken to, especially when the mayor was this furious. She remained with her eyes closed, safe in the calm of her prayers.

The seven-bedroom house revealed no secrets during

their first hour there. Even as Ioli entered the mayor's office on the ground floor, he did not break a sweat. His computer's screen was relatively empty and no files other than family photos and poker games were found.

Ioli decided on a different approach. She watched Oresti Stamos from behind one of the living room columns. *'The eyes never lie'.*

'So, Mister Stamos, ready to fill in that statement, are we?' she asked as she walked over to him.

'Anything to get you out of my house. How can I trust you that it will stay between us? I committed no crime. She is... was over eighteen,' he said, lifting up his head.

'Great. Nothing in your statement will be revealed, unless new evidence is found and you are arrested for Natalie's murder. If you are innocent as you say, you have nothing to fear. Officer Andreou will help you complete your statement,' she said and nodded to Alexandro, who rushed to her side, notepad and pen in hand.

As the mayor was preoccupied with Alexandro, Ioli exited through the kitchen and walked out into the well-maintained garden. She stopped by the tranquil swimming pool and gazed at the house, counting the windows. With her fingers, she separated the long house into rooms.

'Interesting,' she thought and walked back to the modern-day palace. She entered through the open library window, making sure Mayor Stamos would not see her as she made her way back upstairs. She re-entered the master bedroom and spun around 360 degrees.

'Well, well, Mister Bruce Wayne,' she said with a smile. She approached the bookcase by the fireplace and crouched down; her finger running along the deep mark engraved on the expensive parquet floor. She stood up, her hands running around the bookcase. A black button was built-in the back of the third shelf. Ioli pushed it and stepped back, the bookcase following her, revealing a secret room behind it.

The sharp smoky smell from the mayor's Cuban cigars lingered in the thick hot air. The lone window looked unused, an opaque blue curtain blocking most of the sunlight. Ioli switched on the light; a plain light bulb hanging from above.

'*Guess the interior designer was not allowed in here*,' Ioli thought as she looked around, her eyes wide open at the piles of cash, stacked and stacked upon square shelves behind the wooden desk that dominated the room. Ioli sat down on the comfortable-looking office chair and raised the laptop's screen. She placed her USB into place and began to copy various files from the desktop. All were named after dates.

'*What kind of business are you running, Stamos?*'

On the other side of town -the poorer side, some may say- Valentina took less time to search the two-bedroom house with the cozy living room and the small kitchen. All the time under Mrs. Sophia's judgmental gaze.

'Still blaming my Adoni? Still searching for clues to incriminate him?' she had cried as Valentina explained the reason she was there.

'It's not like that, Mrs. Sophia. A case...'

'You should be spending your time finding a good husband at your age. Let the married, more experienced mainland cop solve the case and catch the real killer. You're an islander. It's not proper for a young girl to be single and working...' she said, made a short pause, looked Valentina up and down, and added '... and walking around with so much skin showing.'

'Mrs. Sophia! It's 2016! Now, I am a kind person, but

please, it is too early in the morning to provoke me. Leave the lectures for my mother,' she replied and walked past the elderly lady.

'*It's fucking hot, you old bat,*' she thought, looking down at her pair of jean shorts. '*And, my legs are fabulous,*' she pumped herself up, as she headed to Adonis's room.

She, neither, found anything in the house relating to Natalie.

As she stood thinking how all this was a waste of time - and 'morning coffee relaxing' time, too- her cell phone begun to ring.

'Hello?' she said, bringing silence after her upbeat ring-tone pierced through the air.

'Valentina, dear? It's Maria from next door,' said the middle aged woman who lived by the police station. 'Father Kallinikos is outside the door, looking for you. He's in a right state. I tried to calm him down and he yelled at me to call you immediately. I think you should come, dear. He is going to have a heart attack, pacing up and down in this heat.'

'Thank you, Maria. Tell him I am on my way.'

Valentina did not bother informing Mrs. Sophia of her departure.

'*The sound of my car will let her know,*' she thought, hoping to avoid her begging for Adonis or worse, her so-called advice on how women should behave and dress. 'She probably has flyers with the church's dress code,' Valentina humored herself as she walked out of the one-story bungalow and rushed to her car.

Mrs. Sophia watched her leave from her kitchen window; her eyes peering through the gaps of her patterned, sewn-by-her, white curtains. 'Oh, Lord,' she said, looking at Valentina's buttocks as she ran. 'It should be illegal for shorts to be... well, so damn short,' she said and laughed. She looked around the empty kitchen, realizing how alone she felt. 'He will be home, soon. Tomorrow, he will be home. They have nothing against him. My poor, innocent, little knight,' she whispered and gazed out into the sun. 'Clear skies fear no thunders. Be brave my boy,' she continued talking to herself and did the sign of the cross upon her body. Three fingers of her right hand met, one for the Father, one for the Son and one for The Holy Ghost. They travelled up to her forehead, then to her waist, next to her right shoulder and last to her left. A lonely tear escaped her eye and ran down her cheek, avoiding deep wrinkles along the way. 'Be brave, Sophia. You've been through worse,' she told herself off and decided to blank her mind by diving into her house chores.

Down at the station, Father Kallinikos was still trying to catch his breath. Overweight and a fan of leisure walking, he came down the mountainous road of the church faster than ever before. Pacing up and down was not helping with his breathing or his sweating. Finally, he decided to sit down upon the top step of the police station's entrance. Maria, the neighbor, had given up begging him to come inside and enjoy a refreshing cold beverage.

Father Kallinikos stood up, his eyes on the cloud of dust approaching from the East. Valentina was speeding down the dirt road and even accelerated as the vehicle's wheels touched paved road. The car came to a halt in the parking area, settling exactly between the two parking spots, ignoring the white line separating the two slots. She stepped out of the car, thinking it was just her luck, on the day she risked wearing shorts to meet the priest, especially after Mrs. Sophia's indiscreet *advice*.

'At last, you're here!'

'What's wrong, Father?'

Father Kallinikos looked around at the quiet street. He approached Valentina, placed his hairy hand on her left shoulder and brought his lips closer to her ear. 'The head... Natalie's head, it's... It's in the church.'

Chapter Sixteen

ON BOARD

The island of Syros lay in the Aegean Sea two hours away. Adequate time to put our plan in motion. Syros was the main reason Tracy chose this particular cruise. We had visited the island during our honeymoon, AKA 'the ancient years'. We lived in New York at the time. A far away time when I was an NYPD detective, Tracy was the epitome of the American dream -country girl from the south becoming a top lawyer at a major firm in the city, but most importantly a time when we were called mum and dad. It seems unreal that five whole years had passed already since our daughter's death.

Syros lured Tracy in and a part of her heart remained there. The capital town, 'The City of Hermes' -Ermoupoli in Greek, stands on a natural amphitheatrical site with a wide port to welcome you. From the church of Saint Demetrius, built on the top of the hill towering over the town, down to the calm waters that housed colorful fishing boats, neo-classical buildings, old mansions and white-washed houses cascaded. Along the harbor, taverns and cafes lined up to welcome you with their chairs under the tall palm trees. Tracy's stomach forced her brain to dream of the local dish of salad with capers and the locally-produced San Michali cheese. My brain would never dream of a salad, but it would water my lips with the thought of the Syros Delights (Loukoumia in the local lingo) and the incredible meat dishes served with ice cold beer.

The senior class, all thirty-two of them, followed their teachers to the ship's cinema room. To make sure none left or chose not to participate, the teachers let down their moral walls and agreed on the pupils viewing Deadpool. At least it kept them preoccupied and entertained. Neither of the teachers was amused. By the time the cleverly written opening sequence flashed by before their eyes, the Captain had unlocked their twelve rooms with his master key. He then pulled out a wooden stool from a service room, sat down, stretched his long legs and started to roll cigarettes.

'Do your job, Captain,' he said. 'Nick is on guard at the entrance. No one will come down the hall,' he continued as he licked the thin paper, imprisoning the tobacco, sentenced to burn later on in the evening; enjoyed with a glass of aged red wine. Brought up in poverty, the ship's captain knew well the importance of enjoying the high life his position offered him.

I entered Holly's room, once again. The doctor followed me in. Not one for words, she took a sample of the blood, placed it in a see-through vial and carefully laid it in her cool-bag. 'Nick's a good guy, he just doesn't know how to show it,' she said with a smile and walked out the room. The female mind never ceased to amaze me.

My initial opinion remained intact. There were no signs of a struggle in the room. Someone had studied hard over the *net* to set up the room. Now, if it was Holly or her kidnapper/murderer, I did not know.

I knelt by the large, cloud-shaped blood stain and fell forward upon my hands, to take a look under the bed. A clean empty place stared back. With retaliation from my knees, I lifted myself up and reminisced days of youth, before decades passed and cancer attacked.

The half-empty jewelry box puzzled my grey cells. *'Why take half? And why leave the roommate's valuables behind?'*

Nicole, her roommate, had placed a headless woman's figure with six wiry arms growing out of her, on her bedside table. From the serpent-like arms hung bracelets, a couple of expensive-looking necklaces and a platinum ring.

The girls shared a wardrobe. Neither had had time to unpack and both pieces of luggage stood, side by side, behind the cherry-wood sliding doors. The name tags offered all the information I needed. I pulled out Holly's pink Samsonite suitcase and wondered if it was light because it was empty or had these pricey bags evolved since my day. The top flung open as I pressed the button and witnessed the half empty suitcase. *'Did she bring the blood on board?'* I saw nothing else belonging to Holly in the room.

I decided to open Nicole's luggage as well. The teens chose their own roommates; Mrs. Anne had informed me. Some were pairs of two, most of three. *'Were Nicole and Holly really close? Could she know what's going on or have aided Holly?'*

And there it was. Lying on top of brand-name dresses and designer jeans. A gold bracelet with the name HOLLY carved into it. I dug around the clothes, bags of cosmetics and various shoes, but no more of the missing jewelry was to be found. I slipped the bracelet in a nylon bag and put in my trousers' right-hand pocket.

I exited the room in a rush, nearly bumping into Mrs.

Anne, who came running down the hall. Restless, she could not sit through the movie, knowing about the search ongoing below.

'Just in time.'

'For what?' she asked.

'Who were Nicole and Holly's closest friends?' I asked, stepping back as I had stopped inches from the woman's roundish face.

'The ferocious five,' she scoffed.

'Excuse me?'

She crunched her knuckles; the hair-raising clicking sound vibrated through the narrow walls. She took out her black elastic hair band and pulled her short hair back into a mushroom-like ponytail. 'I blame those brainless American TV movies with the blonde, cool, doltish characters who just want *to be popular*,' she said rolling her eyes. 'The two girls along with Pascale, Karen and Marina drooled over Clueless and Gossip Girl and such, and pretty much looked down on everybody, teachers included. They wore expensive clothes to school and talked about their trips and possessions. Other pupils called them the ferocious five.'

'Did they bully other pupils?'

'No, not in the broadest sense of the word. Maybe a few dirty, degrading stares and an adjective or two, but nothing not heard in every other school. For me, bullying is constantly picking on someone, physically or verbally. The girls never targeted anyone specific. They were cold with all of the others.'

I leaned back on the wall, between two paintings depicting fruit bowls. *'What ever happened to good, old Renaissance replicas and posters?'* My knees were killing me. Even after losing weight, my weak bones could not hold me up for long. 'How about towards one another? Don't these cliques usually have a leader?'

'That would be Nicole. She is the richest out of the five, so I guess that is how their hierarchy is based. I have no idea if bullying occurred within the group or if they had some weird initiation process.'

'I'll have to talk to the girls. Thank you, Mrs. Anne. You've been a great help.'

'Just find my girl, Captain,' she said, turned around and walked off with her palms upon her pale cheeks.

The ship's Captain was gone from his laid-back position; the door leading out to the upper deck betrayed his quick exit for a smoke.

Next door, was the cabin the other three members of the ferocious five shared. The room was tidy and in order. The teens had not had time to unpack most of their possessions. However, all three had unloaded upon their bedside table make-up, fragrances and in the top drawer, their jewelry. Pascale had a marble case with the Eiffel Tower formed on it with Swarovski crystals. Everything inside was silver and platinum. One pair of golden earrings stood out. *'Could it be?'* I used my latex glove-wearing hand and put the earrings into the nylon bag with the bracelet I found in Nicole's clothes. I thoroughly checked everywhere else; my hand travelling around. Under Marina's pure-white pillow, I found a necklace, all tangled up it joined the other two pieces in my evidence bag. Karen's purse hung inside the empty-from-clothes wardrobe. Inside, between an American Express card and a membership card, lay a ring. H&C, 2016 was engraved inside. *'Holly and Chris?'* I thought and dropped the ring in with the other precious pieces of jewelry.

I searched the rest of the rooms with the same meticulous method. '*Boys will be boys*,' I thought with a mischievous grin, as every male pupil had brought condoms with them. Chris had brought condoms with him, too. But, it was not just a first sexual relationship for the youth. He was clearly in-love. Probably defying his mates' laughter, he had placed a photograph of him and Holly by his bed. The hand-made wooden frame held a picture of two happy, excited, and tanned teens holding hands on a beach with their bare feet being caressed by the ocean.

Chris's was the last room I searched. I peeped out into the hallway and saw the Captain mesmerized by his phone. He chuckled every now and then. His wife often complained of his 'YouTube addiction' -as she called it. 'He watches the darndest things. People falling over, cats jumping around, even ships sinking!' she complained to her friends. Here on board, he was free to indulge in his *hobby*.

I closed the cabin's door, remaining inside of the room. My bladder yelled for attention and pushed against my insides. I rushed to the cabin's unfit-for-a-guy-my-size toilet and with one hand on duty, the other flicked through my contact lists. I waited for the drain to silence before dialling Ioli.

'Well, if it isn't the sea-dog, himself,' she said, answering her phone. She tried to sound upbeat, but her voice came across tired and worn-out.

'You back at the office?'

A moment of silence. 'Ioli?' I broke the soundlessness.

'Err, I'm still on the island. Open and shut case, my fat pregnant ass.'

'What? What's going on?'

'I'll fill you in back in Athens. Long story,' she replied, dragging the 'o' in long. 'Special needs prisoned suspect, second dead body, election campaigns. You name it, I've got it. Anyway, screw my troubles. You called to gloat? Having fun? How's Tracy?'

Now, it was my turn to delay to reply. 'Well, not exactly. I seem to have found myself in a situation as well. I have a missing pupil and a pool of what I think to be animal blood.'

'How the hell do mysteries work to find you, boss, I do not know. Poor Tracy.'

'What to do? I must have like an inner magnet or something. Listen, I want a second opinion. We know how a majority of killers take souvenirs from the crime scene or off of the victim. Mostly, serial killers. What are the chances four teenage girls would each take a piece of jewelry of let's say, a presumed victim? A classmate of theirs.'

'Near none. Though there is always a first. If so, we are talking about girls with twisted, violent, abusive pasts. Girls that grew up in a way that would lead to this sort of desire. Could, also, be mimicking from a movie or a book.'

'Could be...'

'Anyway, you said missing pupil. Not dead. The girls are not killers.'

'Yet. A staged scene does not mean no crime. The tokens taken intrigue me.'

'Have you searched the ship? I mean, there are only so many places she could be.'

'I wanted to search the rooms first. Maybe, find her hiding in her boyfriend's room or under one of her girl-friends' beds. I kind of hoped this was all just a prank played on her teachers. I'll get the security tool to help me search the ship.'

'Good luck, boss. I would say let the authorities take care of the situation and get back to your wife, but I know you.'

'I think she is, in a twisted way, happy that I am active. Anyway, I got the bug now. Just like you, pregnant lady. Mark is at home waiting, but there you are.'

'Bunch of work freaks, that's what we are.'

We said our goodbyes and our phones returned to silence. I exited the hallway and nodded to the relaxed Captain.

'Between us, okay? Open the teachers' rooms, too.'

Chapter Seventeen

Ioli's stomach retaliated, having been forced to journey along the uphill, bendy dirt track that served as the lone route to the fifteenth-century church of The Holy Mary. Ioli could feel pieces of chocolate croissant swimming up her esophagus and marching from her neck upwards. Her hand slid across the dusty car buttons in search of the A/C. She pushed it from position three to five and fixed the front grille, allowing the strong cold air to hit her straight on her sweating face.

'You okay?' Valentina asked, leaning closer to her, yet her eyes on the tricky road.

Ioli smiled, and replied that she was. 'Just take it a bit slower round the corners,' she added.

'You're doing better than the priest,' Valentina humored her, making sure she whispered as much as she could. Her mother always warned her that she was lousy at whispering. Her mother had a talent for pointing out all the things Valentina was not good at, in contrast to her father who believed his daughter was a gift to mankind from the

Gods. Valentina did not need to worry about her whispering skills -or lack of them. Father Kallinikos sat in the back, next to Alexandro, breathing heavily and biting his long nails every now and then. Alexandro looked upon the man. He could never understand how priests could cope wearing such thick, heavy, black clothes during Greek summer. As a boy, he used to believe that God provided to the Holy Men the ability to not sweat, to not feel the menacing heat. Something along the lines of his favorite superheroes, the X-Men. Now, as an adult, he found it difficult to trust anything the church had to say. He fought daily to convince himself that Christ and the Bible were perfect and their doctrines had nothing to do with 'the corrupt, unfriendly and judgmental church of today' as he would say during deep philosophical discussions with friends.

Even the police vehicle, having gathered more dust on the way up, seemed pleased to have reached the end of the road. The three officers of the law exited the car at once. Maximus leaped to his feet and begun to bark, showing his sharp teeth through ferocious growls. His master had locked the door and tied Maximus to the handle, ordering him to not let anyone in like a modern-day Kerberos.

The three officers turned to the car. Father Kallinikos remained still.

'Oh, I'm sorry. My mind is a bit lost,' he apologized, finally getting out of the car. 'Maximus, sit!' he said and silence returned to the treeless hill top. 'You must think that I am a right scaredy-cat. I believed I was much braver until today. It's not every day you see a chopped-off head,' he continued as he dawdled, ambling towards his trusted friend. He untied Maximus and unlocked the door, yet did not open it.

'It's on the altar,' he said and walked away from the church.

'Thank you, Father,' Ioli said. 'You are brave. The unusual reaction would have been to not be upset by such a horrific sight,' she continued as Father Kallinikos walked over to the stone brick wall that surrounded the church and sat down upon it.

'Thank you, dear. You're very kind.'

Alexandro had already entered the sacred building, followed by Valentina. Both made a straight line towards Natalie's head.

Ioli paused upon entering. Her right hand played around with her golden chain with the crucifix her grandma had given her on her eighteenth birthday. She kept it in her pocket at all times. Her mind gave birth to guilt, realizing that she had not stepped into a church since her wedding day.

She walked down the newly-installed, red velvet carpet, her eyes scanning around the wooden chairs. No blood stains could be found.

'The head must have been carried in a bag or something of the sort,' she mumbled, her thoughts interrupted by loud clicks echoing from Alexandro's camera.

The flash startled the flies from their morning feast and their buzzing filled the air.

'Locked room. No doors and all windows shut tight,' Valentina said, walking around the room.

Ioli nodded to her and approached the brutally attacked head. 'So much hate...' she said, looking at the stabbed eye sockets. 'The cutting of the head seems to match our knife...' she continued, her eyes examining the neck wound. Ioli, wearing her latex gloves, placed her fingers into the dead girl's opened mouth. 'Nothing,' she spoke to herself as if answering inner questions. Ioli looked up and around. 'Why here? Did the killer wish for forgiveness?'

'Forgiveness?' Alexandro asked. 'By bringing the head?'

'Maybe it wasn't forgiveness for himself, but for the victim,' Ioli replied. 'Bag the head, I'll look around the church, then talk to the priest.'

Minutes later, as Alexandro opened the trunk of the car, a lit cigarette hanging from his bottom lip, and Valentina placed the almost empty body bag inside, Ioli walked over to Father Kallinikos.

'Your eyes seem even more restless than my soul,' the priest said, turning towards Ioli who had just sat down beside him on the low, dusty brick wall.

'Too much thinking,' she replied, with a smile.

'Your only thought should be of the life inside you. A gift from above. Congratulations. Your first?'

Ioli nodded and fondly looked down at her stretched out shirt. 'So, Father, what time did you arrive at the church this morning?'

'Must have been around seven. Maybe a bit earlier. Not sure how long it took me to walk up here. Normally, takes me around fifty minutes,' he answered, removing his jet black, wrinkled skufia.

'And, the church was locked?'

'Yes.'

'And, besides you, who else has keys? I did not notice any signs of a forced entranced.'

An enigmatic smile spread across his face, barely visible among his thick beard. He looked up at the rising sun and wiped his forehead. 'This is a trustworthy place, if not for the tourists we would not bother locking. Many have keys.'

'Why so many?' Ioli looked up at him. She had just opened her notepad and was ready to write names.

149

'The members of the church committee all have keys. They hold their meetings here sometimes. We have churches in the town, but this is our largest and it has offices around the side. Past committee members rarely return their sets of keys...'

'Do you have a list of the members? Do you keep past lists?'

'Yes, yes. Of course. But, I know all the members by heart.'

Ioli underlined her title of COMMITTEE MEMBERS in her black pad, placed the tip of her blue pen on the first line and stared at the priest.

'Oh, err... well, Sakis Stamatiou is the current president...'

'Sakis, the shoe repairer?' Ioli interrupted him, her eyes slightly widening.

'That's the one. Lovely guy. Amazing character. Have you met?'

'You could say so... Who else?'

'My wife is vice-president. I saw her keys this morning, next to mine. The mayor is always on the committee, not that he shows up for most meetings. It's all mostly for good PR really. Same goes for Helen. Ever since she announced she was running for mayor, she joined the committee and has never missed a meeting. You see, we have a vast number of churchgoers here on the island and they all vote. Now, let's see. Who else? Oh, Mrs. Maria, the lady you saw, who lives by the station. She is our treasurer. Oh, and poor Mrs. Sophia. What a terrible thing to go through with Adonis. She is our secretary. But, between us, she is our real president. She has the fire of God in her, that one. A true, modern day missionary,' Father Kallinikos said. 'Our most hardworking member,' he continued, his face relaxed, his mind forgetting the terrors of hours' past. Now, he was just a priest having a talk with a foreigner about the great people of his island.

'*Great! Nearly, all on my suspect list had access to a set of keys!*' Ioli thought.

'How come she wasn't voted in for president? Being so hardworking and all,' Ioli asked, guessing the answer inside her.

Father Kallinikos sat up straight and sighed. 'Mrs. Sophia is an absolute sweetheart. The most ethical person I have ever met. The way she raises that boy, with all his difficulties. Always with him. It's not his fault, God made him just the way He intended to, she always says. But, with a high set of morals, comes high standards. Most women find her to be a tad...'

'Judgmental?'

'Correct. But, she means well. Her seven decades on this planet do not allow her to accept the modern way of life, especially that of women.'

The young priest sighed again and lowered himself from the wall. 'Let me go get you the papers with the past committee members. I will put a small cross by the names of those that have passed away. Save you from looking them up.'

'*Anyone could have their keys, though,*' Ioli nearly said her thought out loud. Yet, she replied with a kind 'Thank you,' and gazed across the serene horizon where the blue sea ran out and met the clear turquoise sky.

Chapter Eighteen

Ioli lay fully-clothed on her hotel bed, her eyes set on the crack running along the ceiling, spreading out like a spider's web around the dangling yellow-light bulb. She kicked off her black orthopedic shoes with the not-visible-by-the-naked-eye heel and sighed out loudly. The shoes, dusty and muddy from the church grounds, fell away with a thud to the floor. Ioli unbuttoned a few shirt buttons and wiped the sweat away from under her beige bra. The soft wet tissue offered much needed relief as it travelled under her getting-larger-by-the-day breasts.

The wall clock struck twelve. *'Midday already.'*

It had been a long day for Ioli's unborn boy. From her early rise, to searching the Mayor's house, to the church and then, coordinating with the coroner's team who came to collect Mr. Sakis' corpse and left with an extra head.

Captain Apostolou travelled with the team. A bull-necked, grey-haired man with a thin cigar permanently attached to his dry lips, he came as soon as he opened his morning email and downloaded the content sent by Ioli.

Ioli felt her eyelids retaliating to her overworked mind and soon, they begun to the take the route of gravity. Their short-lived journey came to an end when Ioli's mind produced one last thought. Her eyes opened wide and with her hands to her sides, she forced herself up. She let the thought swim around for a moment and soon, the puzzle pieces fell into place and her clouds of ideas turned into a storm.

'Well, well, well. Fuck a duck and see what hatches!'

The pregnant woman leapt off the bed and with speed, slipped her sore aching feet into her *sensible* shoes. She ran into the bathroom to empty her bladder for the fifth time of the day. She splashed some cold water on her face and re-fixed her high ponytail. She gazed into the mirror and studied her eyes. 'Let's trust our gut instincts one more time,' she spoke to herself as if someone else; as if giving a lecture to a newbie on the force.

As her hand wrapped around the chipped roundish door knob, she realized her exposed underwear. She buttoned her white shirt, cursing as she had to start again. She was left with an extra button on top and an extra hole below.

She paced down the hotel's hallway, her hand bringing her phone to her ear.

'Hello? Lieutenant Cara?' Valentina's voice came through the speaker.

'Valentina, where are you?' Ioli asked the confused girl. She had dropped off Ioli just ten minutes ago.

'On my way to the station. Thought to complete the paperwork...' Valentina begun to lie in an effort to sound more professional. She was on her way home. Her mother was cooking her favorite dish, fried squid with oven golden potatoes.

'Come back, now,' Ioli said, her heavy breath intercepting every word of the order. 'We are going to your place. I need your make-up and your most revealing dress,' she added, leaving the young officer in a more confused state. '*Or something that fits, at least.*'

Outside, away from the safety offered from the conditioned air behind the glass front-hotel door, Ioli stood under a tilting adolescent palm tree. A foot taller than the wooden fence that surrounded the pool area, a view of careless vacationers rolled out in front of Ioli. With a slight smile, her eyes followed the short skirt, bikini top-wearing waitress expertly carrying a tray of two ice-cold beers over to the white, round plastic table where Alexandro sat listening to old war stories by Captain Apostolou. They accepted their beers with wide smiles -their eyes moving around rapidly, along the curvy lines of the waitress' figure, and ordered lunch.

'Lieutenant Ioli?' Valentina's voice came from behind her.

Ioli was amazed how she did not hear the loud vehicle park just meters from her. '*My thoughts have shut down my concentration.*'

'I wasn't sure if you were pulling my leg. You sounded dead serious,' Valentina said as Ioli entered the car and made herself comfortable beside her.

'I don't blame you,' Ioli replied, turning up the weak A/C.

'So, my house?'

'Straight there,' Ioli answered, leaving Valentina wondering the reasons why.

Valentina turned up the radio and pressed her foot down. Ioli watched as the blonde drove with one heel on her left foot and one brown slipper on the other. 'Oh, I can't drive in heels,' Valentina excused herself. 'My slippers…'

'Hey, I never judge,' Ioli cut her off. Although she did think that the slipper did not work miracles on Valentina's lack of driving skills.

A new scenic route cemented Ioli's belief that Folegandros had to be one of the most picturesque islands she had ever set foot upon. Valentina drove away from the town center and headed through fields of orange and lemon trees, before taking a right towards her own neighborhood. She drove past the two-story house and turned down a narrow dirt track, leading to the back of her yard. 'I basically live in my parent's garden. I fixed up my grandma's old warehouse and outdoor kitchen into a studio apartment,' Valentina explained. 'If we go through the front, you will lose four hours of your life, listening to my mother's endless set of questions and my father's not-so-subtle jokes and theories. If he gets started with politics, we may never leave.'

Ioli chuckled. 'Normal Greek parents, then.'

'Exactly!' Valentina agreed and laughed. 'Do you think we will be like that with our kids?'

Ioli rubbed her tummy and replied, 'I hope not! Poor boy.'

Soon, Valentina locked her blue, glass and aluminium door behind her, glad that her parents were preoccupied watching the opening ceremony of the Olympic Games in Rio and arguing if London's had been more dazzling and exciting.

'London's had James Bond and the Spice girls,' her father said in the only volume his mouth had, loud.

'As if you like either! This has an ecological message. And culture!' her mother contended.

Ioli tried to subdue her shocked look upon entering the spacious studio with the efficient kitchen area and the cozy living room corner. '*So this is what it looks like when a unicorn pukes up rainbows.*' The sheets on the single bed competed with Valentina's nails for most colors blended together. The orange couch clashed with the purple carpet in front of it. The pink curtains made sure you realized a girl lived in the colorful environment with the dozens of animal ornaments. There was a shelf dedicated to frog statues while below it a shelf housed glass pigs, cows and other farm animals.

'May I ask what this is all about?' Valentina found the courage to ask as she opened her burgundy drawers and started to unload her extensive collection of eye shadows and lipsticks.

'I think you better not know. I'm scared you will change my mind. I'm in my crazy place right now and not to show off, but my gut works perfectly in crazy mode. Helped me solve many cases in the past...' Ioli said and paused. 'Leave the make-up for last. Show me your wardrobe. No offense, but find me a dress that reveals legs, back, boobs, the whole works, you know. Your *smuttiest* dress. And, something stretchy. I have to get this baby bump in it!'

Chapter Nineteen

ON BOARD - ISLAND OF SYROS

Disappointing results.

That is exactly how the Chief would react to my investigation so far. That is if he knew about it. Funny, the sense of this much freedom. Not having to delineate back to anyone or fill in endless pages of reports that will be read once and filed away, destined to become a meal for the Homicide Department's large family of basement mice.

After the expected *angry school boy* rant from Nick, he and the Captain, along with a few other crew members searched the ship. The official reason given was one of a lost pet iguana. The Captain was not one for meticulously-crafted excuses, yet it served its purpose. Tourists opened their doors and let a crew member look in the bathroom and under the bed, while scanning 360 degrees the cabin. People on deck or on the bar who asked about what was going on after witnessing crew members searching around, went back to their sunbathing and drinking upon hearing about the unfortunate lost pet.

Disappointing results.

Holly was nowhere to be found.

As for my secret search of the teachers' rooms, all I could say is that Mrs. Anne needed to add more color to her navy blue, grey and black wardrobe while Mr. Zack did not bother hiding his cannabis that well, as it sat upon his brick of a science book. The few grams in the sealed bag were the only amount I found, so I ruled out any chance of him selling to his pupils and classified my find under 'recreational fun for a bored teacher'.

Without a body, and without a documented crime with evidence, the ship docked in the idyllic port of Ermoupoli, the main town of Syros; a place where over twenty thousand lucky Greeks lived. The passengers disembarked and filled the narrow, romantic, quaint streets of the aristocratic town. Among them, the group of pupils and their two teachers. Mrs. Anne wore her bravest face and began the tour she had planned months ago. I had not informed her about my findings in the girls' rooms as keeping the four girls on board while the rest enjoyed the island would appear to be an accusation. They had the right to explain themselves.

The voices that lived inside my head had finished their debate assembly. Logic prevailed over passion; I locked away the case in a dark corner of my mind and returned to Tracy.

'Ready for our date, Mrs. Papacosta?'

She fought to contain her flashy smile as she lifted her head from her book. She took off her glasses and placed them upon her bare crossed legs. 'I never did take your surname,' she replied.

'Tracy Wilson, may I have the pleasure of your company for the next twelve hours?'

'What do you have in mind, smooth talker?'

'As if you haven't planned the whole day out,' I said and approached her laughing. 'Bet you have even written down what we are going to do on each island.'

'Now who is in whose head!' she said and jumped out of her seat. She wore black underwear and as she walked by me, I noticed she had fixed her hair and touched-up her makeup. All she had left to do, was to slide into her short black Versace dress. The one she spent a fortune on and I resisted commenting how could a dress with so little fabric and with more holes than Swiss cheese could be so expensive. Classic guy and fashion case, I guess. The result, though, was something we could both agree on. She looked stunning. Since my eyes first had the honor of seeing Tracy, thirty years ago, she never lost the ability to rock my inner world. People who manage to maintain their love and passion through the years are heroes in my book. Life is never easy, no matter how much advice from self-help books and sites you get and apply. The trick is to ignore the bad as much as you can and focus on the good. Do things that make your heart skip a beat. Do this, do that. All just advice. For me, all that mattered is to have someone to travel along this road together.

'Your eyes are watering up, tough cop,' Tracy said as she placed her soft hand in mine.

'Yeah, the sun...'

'Ssh. Don't ruin it with one of your lame jokes. Let me shower in the love. Girls would kill for a stare like yours.'

Soon, we were strolling in a tangled embrace along the lengthy promenade listening to the sound of the waves and breathing fresh sea air mixed up with kebabs' sweet cooking smell. Relaxed chatter could be heard all around us, mainly from tourists enjoying the serene afternoon. Soon, the aroma of freshly-made loukoumia permeated the air. Our first stop. Sweet tasting. Souvenir shopping followed. I enjoyed my hobby of talking with local shop-owners while Tracy interrupted every minute to show me a plate, statue, coin, snowball, magnet and such. If I nodded *and* smiled, it was a guaranteed buy.

The square behind the main seafront road was the meeting point for the locals. Always one event or another was taking place. We ordered takeout gyro from an Obelix-looking guy in a shop smaller than my bathroom. We took our oily, onion-smelling, delicious street food, known as 'dirty food' here in Greece, and headed to the steps of the neo-classical building of local administration that towered over the square. With watering mouths, we ate while enjoying street performers act and people strolling around.

'Quick, Costa. Finish your food,' Tracy ordered as she leapt up, with a renegade French fry hanging from her lips. I looked up at her with tzatziki-painted lips and mumbled something along the lines of 'what's the rush?'

'The train,' she said and rushed down the steps.

It took me a second to realize she was talking about the made-for-tourists locomotive that ran on a car's engine and carried three blue and white painted wagons with wooden seats behind it. It had no glass fitted on the windows, letting you enjoy the breeze along with the view.

'Proper tourists,' Tracy said as she sat down and held out her phone to photograph my large behind squeezing into a seat. 'Smile,' she said with a grin. 'Smile again, your eyes were closed,' she continued as the train began to roll.

It took us twenty minutes to reach the top of the hill and Saint Demetrius. The stone church was remarkable in its own right, yet it was the view that attracted the flocks of holiday makers. Globetrotters from all over stood and looked down at the charming town with its unique romantic bay. Tracy and I shared a kiss, and that was the last moment my mind wasn't on the case. As our petite train took us back into town and Tracy was ready to surprise me with the restaurant she chose for our wine and dine, I saw the group of the elite school. The four girls stood together, feet from the rest of the group -all with the same bored expression as Mrs. Anne explained the years each building was born in.

I did not let my over-analytical mind ruin date-night and as Apollo dragged away the sun and his sister, Artemis brought a half-moon into the dark sky, two happy, well-fed and verging on drunk fifty-year olds returned to the docked ship.

With the cabin door sealed behind us, pieces of clothing fell to the floor. Naked, Tracy opened the cabin's balcony doors. 'The stars are magnificent tonight. Too many lights in Athens,' she said and walked towards me. I lay on the bed and waited for her lips to travel up my body.

Sex on holidays. I really would love to see a case study upon the subject. I could picture all the graphs and the lines -indicating how times of coitus- travelling upwards and peaking during vacations. Did we always have these hormones and urges, but everyday life tired us down or did the surroundings inspire us to turn our Latin-lover button on?

Tracy's hot body pushing up against mine, switched off my brain from thinking about the subject more. Twenty minutes later, cheerfully exhausted, we shared a pillow, our arms around each other. Tracy closed her eyes, while I secretly craved a cigarette. That was, however, not the last thought on my mind. In the morning, I had to speak with the girls.

The sunrise found Tracy still in bed, stealing back hours of sleep lost due to work. I, on the other hand, peed, scratched, splashed water upon my wrinkle-breeding face, brushed my teeth, dressed in a matter of minutes and headed to the ship's breakfast area. The teachers kept a strict timetable. Eight o'clock sharp all pupils reported to breakfast. I devoured two freshly-baked croissants with my steamy Greek coffee as my eyes studied the students' behavior. The ship had long set sail for Sifnos where the day offered swimming in remote exotic bays.

The four girls sat together at the end of the long table assigned and reserved for the International school. My ears struggled to hear as Holly's name was mentioned by Pascale. Her eyes seemed watery and her fingers played awkwardly with each other. Karen stroked her back. Opposite her, Nicole rolled her eyes and looked away, while Marina continued eating, taking rushed chunks of egg off her porcelain plate. The rest of the students seemed to go about with their vacation without discussing much the disappearance of their fellow pupil.

'*Maybe Holly was not their friend? Maybe she did the bullying? Could I be reading them wrong? There was a chance that their spirits were indeed dampened. Teens should be more lively than this*'. That is when the next thought woke me up better than ten strong Greek coffees. '*Where is Chris?*' Holly's boyfriend was nowhere to be seen.

Mrs. Anne walked around the pupils and was ready to serve herself and join her fellow teacher, when her eyes caught a glimpse of me. I nodded to call her over.

'Good morning, Captain. I was going to come find you after breakfast. My heart has been pounding since yesterday. How did the search go? Secretly, I wished you would call me and say, Holly was hiding somewhere...'

She spoke at a faster pace than my mother when I got into trouble.

The mighty sun appeared to avoid her flesh. Ashen, her thin lips rushed to utter everything on her troubled mind. '... I just managed to control myself and not come hitting on your door last night.'

I smiled and wished her a good day, too. 'Maybe you should eat first,' I advised. 'I, for one, could never function on an empty stomach'.

'Nothing would go down.'

'I found her missing jewelry. Her friends had them.'

'Which one?'

'All four,' I said, and her eyes opened wide. She turned and stared at the girls as I continued 'bring them to the Captain's office, right after breakfast.'

She nodded and whispered a choked 'sure, sure.'

'Oh, and Mrs. Anne?'

'Hmm?' she finally turned back in my direction.

'Where's Chris?'

Ghostly white, paper white, snow white. I thought hard about the word that could describe her color upon hearing my question. Later on, I googled the whitest white to satisfy my raging curiosity. Because white is an achromatic color, a color without color, the whitest white is found on the chitinous scales of the Cyphochilus beetle. They perfectly reflect light from all colors, thus our human eye sees a blazing white color. There; now your mind works as weirdly as mine.

Ten minutes later, the four girls, the Captain and I met in the top-deck cabin that was turned into an office. The room boasted four large square windows with unobstructed views of blue sky. None were open and the room was air-conditioned. However, in the war against the heat wave, the ceiling unit was losing. I guessed Zephyrus blew too strong at such a height for the windows to be open.

The Captain remained seated throughout the conversation and to my satisfaction, silent, too. He stayed behind his antique desk and scratched his two-day beard. He coughed a couple of times, yet I doubt, intentionally. The girls sat in a row; each chair touching the other. Pascale and Karen held hands in the first two chairs, Marina with her eyes fixed on the shining chandelier was next and Nicole sat at the end; the only one with her eyes looking straight at us. I sat my right buttock on the edge of the desk and introduced myself formally.

'It is in my knowledge that you four are Holly's closest friends,' I said and paused to read their expressions. I searched for guilt and yet found none. Not even on Nicole's stern cold visage. 'If you know anything, anything that could help us locate Holly or figure out what is going on, please tell us. You won't be in any trouble whatsoever. On the contrary, keeping secrets from the police is a criminal offense,' I continued and stressed the last two words.

'We know nothing, sir,' Karen spoke with a heavy New York accent. 'Last time we saw her, she was fine. Happier than usual.'

Pascale nodded shakily and agreed. 'Yes, yes. In high spirits as you say,' the French girl said.

Marina's eyes had relocated from the ceiling to the floor and she remained silent. Nicole sat up straight and exhaled deeply, adding tones of drama in her prolonged sigh. 'We already spoke about this between us. We know nothing. She said nothing to us,' she said, complaining. 'We are worried sick. Who would do such a thing to Holly?'

'Maybe a thief after her expensive jewelry,' I said, hoping to read their eyes.

'Yes, maybe,' Pascale agreed again, letting go of Karen's hand.

'Where do you think the missing pieces of jewelry are?'

Silence spread out in the low-ceiling room. I waited and none replied. I turned my gaze to Nicole and raised my eyebrows.

'Why you looking at me? How should I know? That's your job to figure out!'

'Oh, but I have. Four pieces missing,' I said and dropped the bag of bijouterie on the desk in front of them. All four opened the eyes wide and stared at the nylon bag.

'Then why are you asking us about them? Did you catch the thief?' Marina, the only Greek in the group, asked.

'Because I found a piece of jewelry in each of your rooms. One in your bag, one in your box, one in each of your possessions,' I said, my stare travelling from Nicole to Karen.

Their shock and attempts of explanation were silenced by the knocking on the door. As I hoped and thought about all night, it was the doctor.

'Yes?' the Captain called out, reminding us of his presence.

'Good morning, Captain... Oh,' the doctor said and ceased. Her eyes fell upon the flushed startled teens. She turned towards us, leaving the girls behind her back. She dropped a large brown envelope on the desk and mouthed 'it's animal blood' to me. The Captain sighed with relief and wiped his forehead with his arm. I smiled and replied 'thank you.' The doctor returned my smile and left the room. 'I'll go check on Nick,' she said as she closed the door behind her. Nick was ordered by the Captain to assist Mrs. Anne to find her second missing pupil. There was no word of Chris' whereabouts and his phone was switched off.

'So, you are all claiming you have no idea how Holly's jewelry got into your possessions?'

'Exactly,' Nicole said, verging on yelling.

'No idea, sir,' Karen said with Pascale nodding non-stop beside her.

Marina held out her palms in a very Greek way of body language. *I have no idea*, her hands waved.

I tapped my fingers on the wooden desk and scraped my broad jaw.

'Do any of you know Izzy Dix?'

The girls had the same expression I wore on algebra tests. 'Who?' Nicole asked, pushing back her black hair.

'She was a fourteen-year-old girl that committed suicide due to bullying. Holly had handwritten a poem of hers,' I said and paused. 'Was Holly bullied?'

For the first time, their facial expressions showed that they knew something. All of them. They sat up awkwardly, they played with their fingers, they rubbed their legs and their eyes trembled as color slowly vanished from their youthful faces.

'I'll take that as a yes. Bullied by you?'

The three girls turned towards Nicole's direction. Nicole rolled her eyes.

'Oh, bitches, please. As if it was only me. Anyway, it was probably about her mother, not us, so chill.'

'Okay, Nicole. Relax. Slow down. Tell me about what you girls did or said and then about her mother,' I said and sat down on the chair opposite her. I leaned closer to the girl with the watery eyes.

'Holly was... Look, I know how this sounds like to working people like yourself, but in our world it matters, okay?'

I nodded as if I understood.

'Holly was not rich like us. We all come from aristocracy and families that go back centuries. Holly's mother is just a shoe designer that made it big. Not super rich, but enough to send Holly to our school. But, Holly was different. She was not raised rich. She envied our talks about Switzerland and drivers and galas and such. She spoke about things we didn't get. So, sometimes, yeah, we made fun of her. But nothing harsh. We always call each other names. To be honest, she was starting to grow on me. That's why I agreed to share a room with her. To get closer, you know? Get to know her better,' Nicole opened her mouth and let the river flow out of her.

'If she was different why did you let her into your group?'

'My mum forced me. She wanted to get to know Holly's mother and get exclusive designs. But, as I said, Holly wasn't all that bad. I would not call what we said to her as bullying. The world is turning too freaking PC; my daddy always says.'

'And what about her relationship with her mother?'

'Now, that's bullying!' Pascale said.

'How so?'

Karen replied. 'Holly never knew her dad. It was just her and her mama. And that woman would do anything to get into rich circles. She wanted to be treated like a queen. And, Holly with her plain hair, freckled face, extra weight and commoner attitude, did not fit her mother's schemes. She bullied Holly to lose weight, to dress better, to wear makeup at all times and sent her to piano, ballet and a million other lessons. Holly hardly ate or slept.'

'She once told me that she dreamt that her mother would die and leave her in peace,' Marina admitted.

The knocking on the metal door echoed through the room and interrupted my mind processing the chances of Holly's suicide.

'Could this all be to escape her mother? And frame her friends? Or did she leave them a piece of jewelry as presents, as parting gifts? If she did kill herself where is the body? Overboard? Why stage a crime scene? And what about the boyfriend?'

Mrs. Anne stood at the door with Nick and his cold bored expression behind her. She had her arm around Roberto, Chris' best friend and roommate.

'Go on Roberto, tell them,' Mrs Anne urged him.

The Italian licked his lips and with a mischievous grin showed us his phone. 'Chris just called me. He's in Syros. He wants us to turn around and go pick him up.'

'Turn around?' the captain asked in shock.

'What is he doing in Syros?' I asked, standing up.

Roberto raised his top lip. He took a moment to reply.

'He said Holly never showed. He got tired of waiting.'

Chapter Twenty

Mrs. Sophia gazed out of her kitchen window, her hands sunk deep into the soap-filled water that filled the sink. She never left home leaving behind dirty plates. She had just finished eating her small portion of salmon and boiled vegetables. She had served two large pieces of fish with vegetables and rice for Adonis, and covered it with tin foil. The lemon fragrance of the dishwasher liquid competed with the hot apple-pie aroma escaping the oven. She placed the dishes to her side to dry, and opened the oven.

'Perfect,' she said and sniffed the air. The golden brown, sugar coated pie stood proudly before her. She placed it on the table, closed the window, checked for pesky flies and rushed to her bedroom to change into her long black dress. Mrs. Sophia had not worn any color outside of her house since her husband's funeral. She was only twenty-seven at the time and was left a widow with a five-year-old baby girl, Adonis's mother. She never remarried nor even thought about another man. Even if friends tried to persuade her that it was not the horrendous sin that she decided that it was.

'To lay with another man! I'm a widow and a mother!' she had told her mother off for trying to talk her into going on a date with a widower from a nearby village.

The seventy-two-year old woman re-entered her kitchen, opened the top drawer and took out a large sharp knife. She stood above the pie and hoped she had given it adequate time to settle. She, then, began to slice large triangular pieces.

'One for the house, one for Jesus and one for me. The perfect treat for my afternoon coffee,' she said as she cut out three pieces. She looked at the remaining pie. 'Enough for my boy and three cops.'

Just then, the doorbell echoed loudly through the tall-ceiling house.

'I hope it's not Helen, again. I told that sinner that I would vote for her. I can't stand another *vote for me* coffee session,' Mrs. Sophia whispered as she approached the door.

'Hello?'

'It's Lieutenant Ioli Cara…'

Mrs. Sophia waited to hear no more. She pulled the door wide open, her expression revealing her obvious disappointment. 'I thought you had brought my Adonis home.'

'No such luck, grandma,' Ioli commented, chewing gum and walking past the old lady into the house.

Mrs. Sophia's eyes opened wide and scanned Ioli from head to toe. Ioli wore a short red dress, with a deep cleavage and a revealing back. Pregnancy was unable to prevent Ioli from looking dazzling. Dazzling was not the word Mrs. Sophia would have used for the lack of fabric covering Ioli's body. The amount of provocative makeup accelerated the old lady's heartbeat.

'Going to the ball?' she finally managed to say.

'It's my day off today. This is how I always look off-duty. A woman has to work with what the good Lord has so generously provided her,' Ioli replied, pushing up her bosom.

'Well, I must admit, you did not seem this way…' Mrs Sophia said and paused, unsure of how to continue. She did not want to offend the officer in charge of the case that her grandson was arrested for. 'How may I help you, today?' she inquired, wondering about the reason of the Lieutenant's unexpected visit. 'I was on my way over, actually. I've made Adoni some salmon and some apple pie for you all,' she continued, walking into the kitchen.

'Oh, no need for that. I was planning on taking Adoni out for the day, lunch, beach, the whole works.'

Mrs. Sophia stood puzzled by her steamy, apple pie. 'Is that… err… allowed? Proper?'

'Why not? We all know he is innocent. And he is such a sweetheart. What girl would not want a day at the beach with him?'

'I… I…' Mrs. Sophia struggled to form a sentence. Her pale complexion slowly disappeared, giving way to a more reddish one. 'I don't think it is proper to talk like this, Mrs. Cara. You are… what do they call it on those TV shows? You are out of line, that is what you are! I do not like what you are implying here,' she said, the speed of her speech accelerating. Her hands swung uncontrollably and she waved them about as her high-pitched words were released.

'Oh, come on, Sophia. You know how these things go,' Ioli said and approached the round kitchen table. She dipped her finger into the pie and took out a dripping piece of well-baked apple. 'Mmm, delicious,' she said as she licked her finger, wrapping her tongue around it. 'Adoni says he knows all the best beaches on the island. Even the hidden ones. I've heard there is a nudist beach on the east side. I read it is good to soak up as much sun as possible while pregnant…'

'That is unacceptable. There is no way in hell I will allow a whore like you to take my boy to a nudist beach,' the old lady said, banging her clenched fist on the table.

Ioli could not control a slight smile. 'That is quite a temper you've got there, granny. But, bottom line is, fuck you. The boy is an adult. He is eighteen and he is fascinated by me. You know, I've split up with my man and you know how hard it is to raise a child in this bankrupt country. I'm pretty sure Adonis gets good welfare cash…'

'Shut up, you demon!'

Ioli ignored her screams and continued, 'he will fall straight into my arms. He is heartbroken. He really loved Natalie. Hot, steamy, teenage sex with such an experienced girl must be hard to get over.'

'Close your mouth, Lucifer! Shut up! My boy never touched that Babylonian whore. She walked around with her ass and boobs hanging out, opening her legs to every man that smiled at her.'

'Thank God, she's dead,' Ioli said, nodding in agreement.

'Praise His name!' Mrs. Sophia shouted. 'She deserved to die.'

'Is that why you killed her? Did she come on to poor Adonis? That slut!'

Mrs. Sophia took a step back. Her eyes dead still, focused on Ioli's.

'Is that what you think?'

'I don't think. I know. You are *always with him*. You said so yourself, the priest said so and every person I've interrogated mentioned how you always followed him around.'

'I keep him safe from the sins of this world. Anyway, you are just speculating. You have no proof...'

'That's what you believe. You lied about your daughter's death. I looked into it. You mentioned how Adonis was only four when she died. Andreas, Mr. Sakis's son, mentioned how he came to primary school after his mother's death. So he was at least six. Why did you lie? Maybe, because Adoni has memories of you killing her? *Helped* her overdose? You thought if you said he was only four at the time, we would not ask him about it? Besides, after I suspected you, I ask to run your DNA with evidence collected off Mr. Sakis. Guess what? We found your DNA on his clothes. Your sweaty palms touched his shirt when you pushed him off the cliff, did they not? You asked to meet him after you heard his message at the station. You sat outside at that very moment when Valentina played the tape.'

'Screw you, you witch. If you know so much, why don't you arrest me?' she yelled, her left hand crawling across the tablecloth, approaching the sharp kitchen knife by the pie.

'Isn't it obvious? I want Adoni. I am here to propose an offer. I will turn a blind eye to your killing spree and drop the charges against Adoni. In exchange, Adoni and I will marry. With him as my baby's stepdad, my baby will be entitled to welfare, free education, free transport, special treatment. And, you are old, this house will be his one day. On my wage, I could never afford a country house on a Cycladic island.'

'Well, well, well. Look at your true colors shining through.'

'Cut the small talk. What do you say?' Ioli asked, hoping

for a confession. The sensitive tape recorder in her pocket waited for the correct incriminating words to be spoken.

'No, of course. The Lord will never forgive me. Letting his white soul be ruined by your money-whoring ways.'

'And what about your soul? Your murdering ways? Aren't you playing God? Isn't that blasphemy?'

'I kill in the name of the Lord.'

'Is that why you took her head up to church?'

'I prayed for her to the Holy Mother Mary. I left her there to be forgiven. And, I left her body on display for all to see, to prevent other girls from going down that road.'

Ioli felt like praying to the Holy Mother that the recorder picked up Mrs. Sophia's words, loud and clear. 'You have an excuse for everything, don't you? Guess you killed your own daughter to save Adoni?'

The old lady just nodded, her hand laying upon the knife's plastic handle.

'Don't play saint with me. What about Mr. Sakis? From what I've heard he was a good man. What was he?'

'Collateral damage.'

'Fancy words, grandma. Guess I'll have to arrest you as you refused my offer.'

Mrs. Sophia began to walk slowly towards Ioli. 'I like how you think you are leaving here...' she spoke, taking a step with every word. '... alive,' she shouted as she raised the knife in the air, ready to stab Ioli.

Ioli's hands rushed down, pulling out her gun and without hesitation she expertly took a shot. The bullet hit Mrs. Sophia's left shoulder, just by the bone. The force of the shot pushed her back as she leaped to stab Ioli. She flew back and fell on the hard tiled floor.

Crimson blood oozed out of her fresh wound. Her eyes rolled upwards and her body shook violently. 'Heavenly

Father, protect your servant. I pray to you through the Saint of saints, the Holy Mother Mary and through the Holy name of your Son...' she whispered with difficulty. Heavy breaths intervened with her prayers.

Ioli knelt to her side, placing her hands on the wound. She knew well where to hit. A clean shot, through and through. Valentina ran into the house, firearm first. She had been waiting outside, Ioli's orders.

'Ambulance,' Ioli managed to say to her, barely making a sound, completely out of breath.

Valentina replied -in the same whispery manner, that she had already called for the lone doctor on the island.

Ioli's hand ordered her to stay back, out of Mrs. Sophia's eyesight.

'Mrs. Sophia, leave the praying for salvation. I am an expert shooter, you will be dead in minutes. Pray for forgiveness if you wish, but first, admit to your crimes. Save Adoni. With you dead, I will have nothing to save him in court.'

'My boy, my sweet, sweet boy...' she cried.

'I have my tape recorder with me,' Ioli said, taking the recorder out of her pocket. 'State who you are and admit to your sins.'

Ioli reached out and grabbed the half-empty glass on the table. 'Here, have some water.' She lifted the old lady's head with her hand and brought the glass to her dry lips. She let her take a few sips and then pressed down again on her open wound with Mrs Sophia's black head scarf.

'My name is Sophia Papageorgiou and my boy, Adoni is innocent of the crime he is being accused of. I murdered Natalie. She was a whore and the Lord told me to save her.'

Mrs. Sophia took a deep breath and added 'I, also, killed my own daughter to protect him.'

Ioli, then, tied her wound and sat her up upon her legs.

She took a piece of paper from her pocket and quickly wrote the words Mrs. Sophia had just spoken. 'Sign here, too,' she said, placing her blue pen in the wounded woman's hand.

Ioli guided her hand to the paper. A drop of blood fell beside her signature. A dot to end the sentence, to close the bloody case.

'I surrender my soul to your judgment, Lord...' Mrs. Sophia restarted her praying.

'Save it, grandma,' Ioli said, standing up, her hands firmly on the table, helping her with her extra weight. 'You are fine. Get ready for the judgment of the law, first. You are going down for four murders. Natalie was pregnant.'

Chapter Twenty-One

News on Greek islands travel faster than wildfire; could possibly even break land speed records if the gossip was juicy enough. Every family living on Mrs. Sophia's road stood on their balconies and front verandas, among water-deprived flower pots and blossoming trees, watching as Mrs. Sophia was carried out on a medical stretcher, her bare shoulder wrapped with a bloody bandage.

'The cop shot her,' one lady said, wiping her hands on her red apron.

'I heard she murdered Natalie. The doctor's wife told me so,' an obese forty-year old commented as her two boys played with their water-pistols around her.

'She always had a mean streak in her, that one,' a senior man said and continued watering his lemon trees.

The doctor and his nurse wife, accompanied by Alexandro entered the doctor's station-wagon and headed to port. Mrs. Sophia had to be transferred to the nearest general hospital on the nearby island of Naxos.

Alexandro turned and looked at Valentina standing by

her vehicle, her hair floating carefree in the breeze that cooled the high-hilled street. When time is available, we never speak, always waiting for the so-called right moment. Now, with so much left unsaid and not a second to lose, Alexandro sat in the car wondering if he would ever get a chance to speak to Valentina again.

'*I could return for a holiday…*' was his last thought as the doctor drove off and Valentina's figure became one with the horizon.

Ioli sat on a wooden garden chair with a hand-made hay back and drank a glass of water. She held the glass to her mouth and let the ice-cubes settle on her lips.

'You okay?' Valentina asked, standing behind her.

'I'm fine. You know, that woman *fine* that Mark accuses me of hiding so much behind it.'

'So, what would the honest answer be?'

'I'm shit. Dizzy, hot-flashed with a tornado screwing up my stomach. If I was a man, I would lay down for the day and pretend that I was dying,' she said and both women chuckled. 'But, I'm a woman and we've got to go release Adoni,' she continued, standing up.

'Release him to whom?' Valentina wondered, following Ioli to the police car.

'I don't guess you have social services on the island…'

'We only got a second bus last year,' Valentina laughed.

The police car accelerated down the road and the residents of Saint George's street returned to their every morning chores. Having of course already called and informed friends and family about the events that took place in the house at the end of the road.

'I never asked. How are you coping with all this? I know how quiet these islands can be. Not offering much experience. Bravo on handling things so professionally,' Ioli said and watched as a smile came to life on Valentina's tired-looking face.

'If you asked me two days what the most interesting case I had ever handled was, I would have said it was when an owl attacked Christina, the ice-cream lady's hair. She had walked out of Papadopoulos Hairdresser with a weave Amy Winehouse would be envious of and an owl ambushed her.'

'An owl?' Ioli asked, turning to the driver.

'It probably thought her hair brooch was a rat or something and shot down from the sky. Of course, it got its legs caught up in the fake hair. She screamed and screamed, running from door to door. I shouted to her to lay down and stay still as my dad held the bird and I cut her hair. I was quite the local hero for a month or two.'

Ioli laughed and gazed outside the window as they drove down a different colored road. Purple, green and brown doors broke the monotonous blue.

'I miss stories from small villages,' she said, with melancholy echoing behind every word.

'Really?'

'I grew up on a farm house on the outskirts of Chania. I had the best of both worlds. The exciting city and the small community. Both my parents were from small villages and I loved listening to their odd stories.'

The car turned East and the strong sun rays attacked the car; their sunglasses weak to protect them. 'I think you are going to have a few stories of your own to tell after Folegandros. Look,' Valentina said, pointing towards the crowd of around thirty that had gathered outside the police station.

The car passed by them, bringing silence to the gossiping group. The mayor, the priest, Helen AKA the aspiring mayor, Mrs. Maria, the neighbor; the tragic figure of the shoe-maker's wife -held by her son; locals from the square; all the people that Ioli had met over the past two days.

Ioli smiled as politely as she could manage and entered the station. Valentina remained outside, answering multiple questions that were shot at her. Mrs. Maria stood by her, her mind lost in deep thought. Her eyes travelled from Adonis who appeared on the top step of the station to her empty house. Childless, it had been near a decade since she lost her husband.

Ioli had her hand around Adonis's shoulder. The boy was shaken by the news of his grandmother's arrest. Ioli looked at the set of eyes all fixed upon her. In Greek fifty-movies style, she addressed the crowd.

'Adonis is free and cleared of all charges. Know from now on that in no way did he have anything to do with the deaths of Natalie or Mr. Sakis,' Ioli said, fearing the dirty looks the boy would receive for life upon the island. Many had already portrayed him as a killer. No 'innocent until proven guilty' on Aegean rocks. She paused unsure how to continue.

'Adonis, I have good news for you,' Valentina spoke and approached the young man. 'Mrs. Maria wishes for you to go live with her.'

'I need the company,' Mrs. Maria added, a sincere large smile gracing her face.

The boy looked unsure; his eyes fixed on the ground. 'I want my nanna,' Ioli heard him whisper from behind closed teeth.

'Well, on behalf of our small community I believe great thanks are in hand to the officers...' the mayor begun speaking loudly and took a few steps forward as to be seen by all. Mrs. Helen rolled her eyes. 'I can't believe he is going to turn this into some sort of success on his behalf,' she told her daughter who stood behind her chewing gum, thinking how she would rather be at home watching her favorite show than here with her nagging mother.

The mayor walked up to Ioli continuing his pompous speech. He avoided shaking Ioli's hand; her icy look kept him at bay.

'... a happy end to a tragic story...'

'A happy end to all, but you, mayor,' Captain Apostolou interrupted his speech, passing through the crowd that seemed to be growing larger as the news travelled around town. He took out his pair of handcuffs, spat his cigarette to the ground and placed his right hand upon his gun. 'I have a warrant for your arrest.'

'My... my arrest? What for? Sophia has been arrested...' the mayor spoke, maintaining his speech tone.

'For drug trafficking,' the captain replied. The mayor's face froze on the spot. 'We have all the evidence we need, found on your home computer.'

'Now, that's a happy ending,' Ioli said as the police captain locked the mayor's hands in the cuffs.

'Indeed,' Helen said, her entire body gloating.

I wish I could say that this was indeed a story with a happy ending.

But life is not one for fairness and 'should haves'.

Adonis never stopped asking for his grandmother. As Mrs. Maria placed her hand gently around his and invited him into her home for chocolate cake, Adonis let out an animal-like scream. He pulled away and ran down the street, ignoring the calls from his fellow villagers to come back. Ioli rushed behind him, panting, her right hand under her tummy.

'Take it easy, I'll catch him,' Valentina told her and remembering her high school track days, she chased the youth until he reached the caldera. Valentina cautiously took steps towards Adoni who was standing on the wall, looking down the two-hundred meter drop.

'Adoni, relax. You will see your grandma soon. Come down from there. You know Mrs. Maria. She is a kind old lady and an amazing cook...'

'All... my life... people have called me dumb... I... I know Nanna is going to prison,' he yelled. 'I have no one,' he added calmer now, and those were the last words he ever spoke. He let his body fall, disappearing from Ioli's eyesight as she arrived behind Valentina. Exhausted, she knelt to the ground and wept.

Mrs. Sophia heard the news an hour later.

Her body and mind could not cope with the loss of Adoni and a stroke left her comatose. A second stroke during the night finished her off.

A deadly ending to a murderous cycle.

Chapter Twenty-Two

'Case closed. Big fuck up. Waiting for the police ferry to get off this damn island. Hope things are better your end. Kisses to Tracy.'

Ioli's message read like a telegraph when I awoke that morning. I did not bother to reply as much was on my mind. I had rushed to breakfast, noticed Chris missing and went to the Captain's office to interrogate the four girls.

Now, Roberto stood opposite me, informing me that Chris was still in Ermoupoli, back in Syros.

I picked up my phone and dialled Ioli.

'Please still be there, please still be there,' I talked to myself as I walked out of the office, past evil-eyed Nick and into the long hall.

'Yeah, boss?' Ioli's voice came through after what seemed to be centuries.

'Where are you?'

'Folegandros. I'm getting ready to leave. Didn't you get my text?'

'Thank God. Listen, I know it may be much to ask for you, pregnant, tired and all, but get the ferry to come get me from Sifnos.'

'What? Why? What's wrong? Why do you want to go back to Athens? Aren't you feeling okay?'

'We aren't going Athens. We are going to Syros to pick up a boy. We are going to solve my case as well,' I shouted into the phone. Joy, testosterone, excitement; I could not tell. But my heart was glad to be back in the game.

The cruise ship entered the bay and approached Kamares beach, one of the finest beaches not only Sifnos, but the entire group of Cyclades had to boast. Its turquoise, swimming-pool-clear waters enticed the passengers to dive in. Blown-up boats were prepared by the crew for passengers wishing to enjoy shallower waters and lay on the sandy beach. 'A perfect option for kids and sun-soakers,' the Captain defined it.

The Captain, also, thanked me a dozen times for calling the police ferry and avoiding the commotion of the ship turning back to Syros. Truth be told, the ferry would take a fifth of the time. Tracy, on the other hand, was not that thrilled.

'Baby, you will sunbathe for a couple of hours, have a swim and I'll be back shortly. Sit with those chatty ladies that we met last night. I'll be back before you know it,' I promised.

Tracy crossed her arms and her eyes shot me straight in the face.

'You better be back on time, Papacosta or I will be sitting with the young tall Brazilian guy we also met on board. Pedro, I think he was called.'

I smiled and kissed her on her sealed lips. 'See you in three hours, tops.'

'Go. Get. Go be the hero, babes.'

At that moment, the loud engine of the crashing-through-the-waves speed boat of the police was heard and we turned to see it approaching the ship from a distance. We stood in the ship's open cavity that served to unload cargo. The ferry swayed and came to our side. Ioli stood opposite us, her hair blowing in the wind.

'Darling, you are the most fabulous-looking pregnant girl of the high seas,' Tracy jokingly shouted.

'Tell that to the crew who just saw me puke all over their deck!'

I stood there with a smile. It never ceased to amaze me, how much I missed her. To stand once again side by side heading to solve a case was a main 'keep-going goal', during my fight with cancer.

I kept Ioli up to date on what was going on and who Chris was.

'So he was supposed to meet the girl?'

'It seems that way. A teen elopement story...'

The waves crashed ferociously against the ferry and fat drops of water splashed against us. Soon, the compact town of Ermoupoli rose from the horizon, shining under the blazing sun. I called Chris on his cell phone and instructed the upset boy to meet us at the dock.

The lanky youth paced up and down the dock with his hands sunk deep in his beige shorts' pockets, raising his head every now and then at the boat.

'Chris, I am Captain Papacosta. We met on board. This is my partner, Lieutenant Ioli Cara.'

The word partner sent shivers down my spine. I felt as if I had not missed a day away.

The three of us sat down on a cozy, wooden, green bench by the sea. Ioli brought over cold beverages from the small kiosk across the road. She, also, bought an extra large bag of jelly babies.

'Chris, we know that it was animal blood in Holly's cabin. Were you two planning to run off together?'

He nodded his head and wiped his nose with his hand. 'We were supposed to meet behind the administration building. You know, the big one, in front of the square. I waited for hours. She never showed.'

'Why all the blood and staging?' Ioli asked, swallowing her third jelly baby. A helpless yellow one.

Chris gazed at the ever-moving sea. 'Holly said she needed to escape her life. Her mother. I never knew she meant me, too,' he said, picked up a round white pebble and threw it with force into the high waves.

'She wanted people to think she was dead?' I asked.

'Exactly,' he replied and threw another pebble. A black one this time. 'She Googled all about it. How to stage your death. We planned this for months. Bought pig's blood and everything. She wanted to be declared dead.'

'Why the jewelry?'

'Revenge. She knew it was a long shot, but she wished the four cows, that's what she called them, to be blamed for her death. I helped her and she ditched me. Left me standing here like a fool.'

'What was going to be your plan? I mean, you were going to leave your life behind, too,' I asked.

'My plan? My parents don't give a shit about me. I was going to call them and tell them that my girlfriend died and I was so devastated that I was going to take a year or two off to travel. My mum never wanted Holly with me anyway. A white girl. She always moaned how these white girls were taking good black men. And my dad? He would be glad to have his fuck-up son out of his way. He deposits me five thousand Euro per month as my allowance. Plenty for me and Holly to live happily somewhere exotic.'

'How will Holly live, now? Did she have money? Where did you plan on going next?'

Chris shook his head. 'No money. Her bitch of a mother checked where every last Euro was spent. As for where we were going, Holly always dreamt of Japan. She was fascinated by their culture. We were going to pay a fisherman to take us from here to the Turkish shores. Holly bought us fake passports off the internet. You can order anything these days. And from Turkey, Japan.'

And there it was. The plan of a girl in pain.

Our plan was simple. Get the coastguard to check all fishing boats, interrogate all local fishermen, have the local police search the island with photos of Holly and inform the Turkish authorities to stop a Miranda Smith, aged eighteen; Holly's fake passport according to Chris.

The case was assigned to Captain Nerantzi of Ermoupoli police department.

I returned to Tracy's tanned body within my promised timeframe and Ioli to Mark's strong arms, back in Athens. Her much deserved maternity leave began the second she stepped off the police ferry.

Every day, I hoped for news. News that never came.

Even when we returned home after our ten-day cruise, I still anticipated a resolution. I had called Ermoupoli's police department every day of the cruise and received the same answer of 'nothing new' and 'no sign of the girl'.

'I wish life was sometimes a movie or a book and there was a happy fairy-tale ending to Holly's story,' I told Tracy as she unpacked our luggage and I fell, face-down, upon our king-sized bed.

'I'm sure everything will turn out just fine in the end,' Tracy said and lay upon my back.

Her words could not have been further from the truth.

Chapter Twenty-Three

ATHENS

Three months later

September, or as I prefer to call it, 'the fourth summer month', finally came to an end and gave place to a cooler likable October. Rain was of course still out of the question, yet scattered clouds defied the mighty sun and fought to cover the gloomy sky. October the eighth was a glorious day.

My return to active duty.

I left home in a hurry and silently, as to not wake Tracy. She would have made a big deal out of it. Yet, it was a big deal. A peculiar feeling floated in me. I was a cancer survivor. On one hand, you want to feel proud and mighty for your accomplishment, on the other guilt and weird thoughts take over. Why me? Out of all the thousands that die daily, why did I survive? Why not the mother of three? Why not the nine-year-old boy?

I drove my Audi into the underground parking of police headquarters and waved to the group of officers smoking by the elevator; it was like not a single day had passed since I left. The only difference was the wider-than-before smiles I received.

I stood alone as the metal cage lifted me up. The mirror opposite me revealing the sweat on my forehead. Anxiety mixed with joy. I wiped the salty droplets away and smiled at the few hairs growing out of my scalp. Ding. The doors opened and I turned to exit on the floor that housed homicide. I found myself below a huge WELCOME BACK CAPTAIN sign and opposite me stood a crowd of clapping co-workers. On the bright side, they had bought galatompoureko, the King of all things sweet, here in Greece.

October the ninth decided to challenge the previous day and become more memorable in my mind's inner calendar. I sat in my corner office and was reading old cases from the previous year, slightly disappointed at the lack of clapping and cakes this time around.

Suddenly, my phone went into earthquake mode and began trembling across my desk. Tracy's winsome face with her endearing little grin flashed on the screen.

'Hey, babe. Wake up okay?'

'The baby is coming!' Tracy yelled.

'Really? Okay... err...'

'Just leave work and get your ass down to the clinic. I'm on my way, now. Love you,' she said and I pictured her running out the house to catch the bus.

I grinned as I closed the office door behind me. Second day back and I was already taking a day off.

Miles away, in a three-story private hospital, Mark drove into his work's parking space. It was his first time not rushing to his office, but to the gynaecology department. A nurse waited for them, wheelchair by her side.

'Good morning, doctor. Just as you requested,' she said as she handed him the modern-looking wheelchair.

'Oh, for fuck's sake, Markie. I can walk, you know,' Ioli complained, her hands steady upon her ready-to-explode tummy.

'Yes, but you don't have to,' he replied and leaped out of the car, running to her side. He wheeled his wife through the glass doors and turned right.

'Everything is gonna be just fine. Great even,' he said.

'Talking to me or yourself?' Ioli commented, in a more relaxed manner.

Mark chuckled and replied, 'to myself of course. You are a monster of serenity.'

'Now, that's a new one. I will remind you of that next time you cry that I drive you crazy and how women are the root of all evil.'

Even the nurse could not resist laughing.

By the time Tracy and I entered the hospital, Ioli was in the delivery room, being told to push by Dr. Eva Karezi. We waited patiently outside.

'You know...' I said, 'when I was a kid, I used to think that the delivery room was somewhere food was prepared for takeaways.'

Tracy shook her head and sighed. 'I expected nothing less from you, dear. The majority of your mind is occupied by thoughts of food.'

I placed my hand upon hers and squeezed it. 'Remember when...'

'Don't.'

I left it at that. 'Do you think Ioli had time to call her mother?'

'Well, she called me. I would believe she called her mother first.'

I pulled out my phone and dialled Mrs. Anna's number.

'Costa!' her Greek, jovial voice came through. 'I've heard!' she yelled, her voice struggling against strong winds. 'I'm on the ship. I arrive at the port in eight hours. I will go mad by then. My first grandchild!'

'Can't wait to see you, Mrs. Anna. Try to relax. Are you alone?'

Her laugh conquered the wind and came through loud and upbeat. 'America ruined you, boy. Of course not! It's me, my sister Yianna, my four first cousins, two second cousins, my neighbor Kyriaki, Polina -Ioli's best friend, with her two kids and my late-husband's mother. We're Greek. We gather quickly for weddings, funerals and births!'

I was re-telling the list of travellers to Tracy when the door opened and out came the short nurse with the curly hair. We both stood up immediately.

'All went great. Healthy baby boy. Mother is doing great,' she said in 'nurse language' of telegraphic sentences. 'Not so sure about the father, though,' she giggled. 'Never seen the doctor so stressed,' she added, and wandered down the white chlorine-smelling corridor.

'Can we go in?' Tracy called before the red-haired nurse vanished from sight.

A word similar to 'sure' echoed through the narrow walls. '32C,' sounded clearer. Tracy did not wait for any other confirmation and rushed into the elevator. Women and newborn babies; same excitement as men and flashy new motors. I know, I am stuck in the fifties, yet never lived in the decade.

An image to melt the toughest soul. Ioli glowing in delight with a bundle of a new arrival into this world. Two piercing greyish-blue eyes escaped the blanket.

'He looks just like you,' Tracy said. 'No offense, Mark,' she added, turning to the exhausted-looking father.

'None taken. A boy as beautiful as Ioli? Now, there's a heartbreaker in the making,' Mark joked, gently caressing his wife's messed-up hair.

'Oh, God. What have I gotten myself into?' Ioli asked.

'That's nothing. Just wait. Your entire family has taken over a ship and are headed our way,' I informed her. 'I spoke with your mother.'

'Let's enjoy the peace while it lasts then.'

'You're a mother now, dear. Forget peace for a very long time,' Tracy said and sat down on the bed, stroking Ioli's leg.

Our laughter was interrupted by knocking on the door. Two familiar faces appeared, blue teddy bear and flowers in hand.

Alexandros and Valentina smiled widely at us. 'Sorry, for coming so soon. Valentina said first day is for family, but we were nearby when I called work looking for you, Captain Papacosta, and Mary told me you had left as Ioli gave birth. Congrats, partner.'

'Thank you, Alexandros,' Ioli replied and introduced the two to Mark. 'So, you two...?' she asked with a grin.

'Yes,' Valentina replied. 'Alexandros managed to find me a spot with the traffic police, here in Athens. Tiring, but at least I left the island.'

'But at least, I'm with Alexandros!' he said and chuckled. 'That's supposed to be your answer.'

'Whatever helps you get through the day, honey.'

Chapter Twenty-Four

The sun held a serious grudge against the town of Ioannina, in the northern part of Greece. While a daily lover to the islands and capital for most of the year, the sun took days off when visiting Yiannena -as it is more commonly known. Cloudy days were all November had to offer. Clouds and rain exchanged places throughout the day, keeping citizens behind closed doors, safe in the warmth of fireplaces and radiators.

Sixteen-year-old Tina Lehou hated the depressing weather as she referred to it. She came home from school, ate whatever her single mother had prepared, finished her homework and sat on her bed with her phone in hand. A summer person, Tina often cursed her luck for being born in such a wintery town. The way things were going this year, snow could arrive as early as Christmas.

Tina sighed, day in, day out, until December arrived and offered the first proper sunny winter day. It was a Saturday and Tina awoke with a smile as the sunrays penetrated her thin pink curtain and illuminated her once dark room.

Tina kicked back her heavy blanket and woollen sheets, and leapt off her single bed. Her purple pajamas with the yellow triangles fell quickly to the floor. Her body welcomed her cherished red Adidas tracksuit and her natural blonde hair was pulled up into her a high ponytail. Tina opened her screeching door slowly. As always, her mother had returned home late and weary. Tina grabbed a juicy-looking, lawn-green apple and exited her family home. The streets were quiet at such an early hour. Just a few elderly ladies sweeping the front of their homes and a few walking their dogs, who eagerly sniffed around in search for the ideal spot to release bodily fluids. Tina placed her earphones on and pressed play on her phone. With Taylor Swift as company, she began to jog down the serene road, heading towards the majestic lake of Pamvotis.

Tina picked up her pace as she approached the castle walls that surrounded the old part of town. She ran upon bricked pavements and with a smile, she reached the calm waters of the large lake. She paused at the pier, took a deep breath and stretched out her arms. The sun had fully come into sight, sneaking out from behind high mountains that kept the city imprisoned in the great valley. Tina looked left and right, trying to decide which way to choose for her morning run. She remembered that last time, she had taken the scenic route towards Perama Cave. Without a second thought, she headed in the opposite direction. 'The peaceful route'. Alone, she jogged by the lake, silently singing along to her favorite music. A mile into her run, her eyes noticed something familiar. 'Deja vu, my ass,' she said, noticing the blue van passing by on the road above. It had passed by three times already.

Tina had seen it before. Last week. Twice outside her school and once a few houses away from hers. She began regretting not telling her mother or her teacher and for coming out for a jog alone. She decided to leave the quiet path and head upwards, back towards the town.

'*It is half past seven already and more people should be out and about*'.

Tina wiped her forehead, turned off her music and ran towards more crowded streets. With frantic looks behind her, she reached her first destination. The kiosk of Mr. Stefanos by the castle walls. She took her time, taking a bottle of water out of the fridge and taking it up to the petite window, where Mr. Stefanos served his customers. She wished him a good morning and started to discuss the weather. She stayed at the kiosk for a good ten minutes; her eyes always fixed on the road, checking for the blue van. It did not show.

Relieved and with her heartbeat returning to normal rates, she began to jog for home. As she turned by the tall brick wall, two arms came out from behind the castle gate and pulled her into the shadows. A hand fell hard upon her mouth, drowning her attempts to scream. A needle penetrated her neck's pale skin and in less than a minute, Tina's eyes felt heavy and fell closed.

She awoke later; her head suffering worse than after her birthday party's hangover. To her horror, everything remained dark. A thick oily cloth covered her eyes. She tried to move, only to be restrained by the chunky rope that surrounded her wrists. Tina pulled to free herself, but it was futile; the rope only cut deeper into her pale skin, leaving red fresh bruises as she struggled. She kicked around, yet her legs hit nothing around them. She sensed she was on something soft, like a mattress.

'Oh, God, oh, God. Please,' she repeated, before deciding to scream for help at the top of her lungs.

In the front seat of the van, the tall man had squeezed his sweaty cheek upon the cool glass window. He lit another cigarette and turned up the stereo; his half empty bottle of whiskey sat by his side.

'What a wonderful day,' he spoke to himself as he blew out heavy smoke into the confined area. He listened to the entire song, before stepping out the vehicle and heading to the back.

Tina heard the clanking of the van doors as her attacker opened them. Weak sunlight reached her eyes, brightening the cloth that blocked her vision.

'Please, sir. Let me go...'

'Shut up,' he replied as if bored with her.

She shivered as she felt him sit upon her. Tina screamed again, only to be slapped hard across the face.

'No one can hear you up here, princess, but I don't want a headache,' he mumbled and proceeded to stuff her mouth with an old sock.

The sound of scissors was the next thing Tina heard. One by one, he ripped off her clothes, leaving her naked, vulnerable and more terrified than ever before. The scissors did not stop there. The whiskey-smelling man lay upon her, sniffing her hair like a hound after a fox. He cut locks off her blonde hair and brought them to his nostrils. He sniffed them as he fondled his privates.

Tina then, sensed his hand travelling along her leg. Soon, his fingers were inside of her. A virgin, Tina yelled out, only to be choked by the dirty sock. Tears fell freely, forming streaks upon her cold teenaged face. As the strong man had his way with her untouched body, Tina thought of her mum, her friends, even her school. Any thought to escape the ordeal her body was going through. Soon, the beast upon her grunted in delight and Tina prayed it was over.

She was not as lucky.

The man swiftly turned her over. He massaged her back, licking it every now and then.

'Perfect,' he whispered into her ear and bit down on her earlobe.

He, then, took the sharp scissors in his hand and began to carve into Tina's back. The pain was excruciating and unreal. Pieces of skin were pulled back and bloody lines formed across her body. Blood oozing out only excited him more as he continued with his devilish drawing.

'Number five, woo,' he proudly announced as he stared down at the bloody, gaping wounds that formed a five on her back.

'Good bye, princess,' he whispered again into her ear.

The last thing Tina ever felt were the scissors piercing through her neck. With laughter, the man pushed them into her neck and with eyes wide open, he twisted them around. Tina lost consciousness and her last breath departed from her horrified opened mouth.

The man yanked out his murderous weapon and licked along the razor-sharp blades. He looked down at his watch.

'Excellent. Plenty of time,' he said and began to rape her lifeless body again.

Late that night, he dumped the abused body into the lake. He drove up to the edge of a remote cliff, bordering the deep lake. He wrapped the bloody body in a large plastic bag, threw in ten large scoops of freshly-made cement from his green bucket and sealed it off. He lifted the bag into his strong arms and with ease, dropped her from above.

Whistling, he drove home, parked, ate, had a shower and feeling relaxed, he went to bed.

Tina's mother did not have such peace of mind as to relax, never mind sleep. She spent all day looking for her daughter, calling all her relatives and friends.

As the blackness of the night rolled in, she called the police. As she waited for the police to arrive, she did something that she thought she would never do. She opened her daughter's diary. Among private thoughts, there it was. Tina's description of the van that she sensed following her that week. Among her teenage opinions, she had noted down the van's license plate.

An hour later, to the shock of his mother, girlfriend and neighbors, the tall man was arrested and his van taken into evidence.

Chapter Twenty-Five

ATHENS

A week before Christmas

'Come on, Grinch. One more shop,' Tracy teased me. 'At least, it's nice and cold, and raining. I deserve a smiling face after listening to you complaining about the freaking heat all summer long.'

She had a valid point. I hated the scorching heat waves and longed for winter. My skin's pores craved and devoured the chilling air and the drops of fresh rain. I enjoyed the lack of sweat stains on my shirts and long nights of hot chocolate drinks in front of an entertaining movie. The only dispiriting period of this glorious season was Christmas. The endless shopping, the glued-on fake smiles, the commercial exploitation, the bright lights and the endless horror of Christmas tunes and carols on repeat.

'There,' I replied, flashing my teeth at my bag-carrying wife.

'Keep it on,' she ordered and yanked my hand, leading

me into the next department store. 'Behave and I'll buy you some mini-donuts.'

'You talk to me like I'm a five-year-old.'

'Men and dogs,' she laughed and proceeded with her hunt for new shoes to wear on New Year's Eve. Tracy had a theory that women should talk the same to their men as they talk to their dogs when complimenting them.

I placed my hands deep in my pockets and wandered around the store in search for a comfortable place to sit down. Opposite me, another tired husband sat on a navy blue sofa, outside the changing rooms, reading his news-paper app. With Jingle Bell Rock booming over the radio, I sat beside the young man with the freckles spread out below his dark eyes. Discreetly, my eyes fell upon his tablet and I read the news titles with him. Crisis, crisis, crisis. The monotony of subjects during the festive season. High prices and low wages.

The short man sighed and lowered his device, getting ready to close it and drop it by his side.

'No effin way!' I shouted, startling the guy and the few shoppers around us. I stood up and took the tablet into my trembling hands. Front page and a familiar, cocky, arrogant face stared back at me. 'Nick Pavlou,' I said to Tracy, who rushed to my side. 'Look!'

Tracy's mouth opened wide and her jaw journeyed down. 'Rape?'

'And not just a one-time offender. They matched his DNA to unsolved cases spanning back over the years. I have to call Ioli,' I said, gave the tablet back to its shocked speechless owner and marched out of the crowded store.

Tracy waved goodbye to the wall of high heels and dashed behind me. By the time she reached me, Ioli had picked up the phone.

'... I have a bad feeling about this. I never trusted the guy. I have to go. I have to ask...'

Chapter Twenty-Six

ATHENS TO IOANNINA

Thankfully, the new road system was finished before the economic meltdown that stopped all development, here in Greece.

The nine-hour journey to Ioannina had been cut down to six due to new roads that stubbornly cut through mountains to connect smaller towns to the bustling metropolis of Athens.

Ioli drove as my heart could not stand still long enough for me to focus on the road.

'How could I have missed something like this?'

'Wolves in sheep's clothing,' Ioli replied, her mind on Adonis's grandmother.

'That's the thing. He was no sheep. He was an arrogant, unhelpful...'

'You could list ten pages of adjectives, boss, but none of them pointed to rapist and killer. There was no evidence at all against him. That is, if he murdered your missing girl.'

I sighed and looked out of the window. 'Even the

weather is in a mood today,' I commented at the semi-cloudy sky. Patches of light fell across cows carelessly eating fresh grass in the meadows around us. Behind them, above the mountainous horizon, black clouds began to gather and conspired to rain later on in the evening.

'I'm done with mood swings,' Ioli chuckled.

'Wait until your next pregnancy.'

'Next? You must be mad.'

'Why do all new parents say so? Just wait and see,' I said and stretched my hands, clicking my finger knuckles. 'Thanks for coming, by the way. How did Mark take it? You are on maternity leave after all.'

'Mark is at work. My mum is with the little terrorist of love.'

'Terrorist of love!' I could not help but laugh at loud. 'I've always said you're a weird one, Cara.'

'At least, I can make you laugh at times like these,' she replied as she overtook the slow-in-the-fast-lane car in front of us.

An hour later, the imposing Rio-Antirio Bridge filled our horizon. Its tall pylons with white cables stood resembling still ships in the wild waters.

'You know, with better money management this country could flourish,' I said.

'Well, tell us something new,' Ioli replied as she turned to enter the 2,880-meter bridge.

I paid the tired-looking man the thirteen-euro toll and wished him a good afternoon. He grunted something about his shift having four more hours to go and ordered me in a bored voice to move along.

We drove in silence, locked between the endless sea on our left and green hills on our right. The air rushed in the moving vehicle; pure, fresh. The countryside as always, divine.

The town of Agrinio offered our only stop. A run-in gas station and a fast-food joint were all we needed. We ordered six Greek gyros; Ioli being the only woman I have ever met who was capable of devouring three. Slices of pork and chicken covered in devilicious tzatziki sauce descended down our esophaguses and fulfilled our need to eat. Cold sodas journeyed behind them and after a visit to our respective restrooms, the open road welcomed us once again.

We switched seats and radio stations. I love her, but her fondness for girl-power ballads will be the death of my eardrums. If she could only resist from singing along; if only.

Hours later, we began the downhill drive to the once great Byzantine town of Ioannina. Trapped between snowy mountains and a lake, it was candy to a visitor's eye. Not that my restless mind could focus on the spectacular view.

We had already gone over procedural hustles with the officers in-charge of Nick's case and were permitted to visit and interrogate him.

The high gates of Ioannina Prison moved back and the guard showed us to the visitor's parking area. The air carried the smell of freshly-cut grass and the skies above us rumbled in delight. By luck, we avoided the fat drops of water that plummeted down as soon as we entered the dull-looking grey building.

The vast visitor's room was deserted; preserved just for us. We chose a table in the middle and sat side by side. Above us, a guard leaned on the rusty rails like an eagle overlooking its territory. The massive window to our left, filled with droplets, offered unobstructed views of wastelands heading up to the towering rough mountains.

Our coffees arrived before Nick Pavlou.

His horrific smirk entered the room during my third sip.

'Well, you're the last person I expected to see,' he said, as two beefy guards escorted him through the room. 'Now, who's this pretty thing?' he said as he sat and turned his attention to Ioli.

'I'm a bit old for your likings, aren't I?'

'I love exceptions. Confirms the rule and all,' he replied, leaning forward on the cold metal table. His cuffs rattled as he raised his arms and placed his hands, palms down. 'So, what's up, mighty know-it-all, Captain?'

'Cut the crap, Nick. I was served enough of it on board. Enjoyed your little game, did you?'

He lifted his hands up high as if to say '*I don't know what you are talking about*', leaving sweaty prints on the table's hard surface.

'Clueless is not your style. You numbered them. They have you down for four murders already. Four teenage girls, Nick. You are getting life in prison. What do you have to lose? Is Holly the missing number four?'

He remained silent; his eyes never leaving mine.

'What's in it for me?'

'Closure for the girl's family.'

'Oh, please, Costa. Her whore of a mother was the reason she was running away.'

'So, you did speak with her?'

'Could have heard it from the rest of the kids,' he replied, lowering his tone and pretending he was bored with me.

'He is right, boss. Fuck the family,' Ioli said.

'Ooh, I like this one,' Nick said and widened his crooked smile; his yellowy teeth peeking through his newly-prison-grown beard.

'Do it for you, Nick. You told a story. From one to five. Without Four, your tale is unfinished, incomplete. You will be forgotten, locked up as just another rapist slash killer. But tell your story to a reporter, your whole story and you earn immortality. Probably get a cool nickname. Nick, the virgin slayer. That was the reason you chose them so young, right? Licked them up and down. Innocent and pure, lost under your skilful hands...'

'Stop it, woman. You're arousing me,' he said and let out a loud sinister laugh.

'People will look up to you in prison,' she lied. 'Successful serial killers gain respect inside. The more victims, the larger the respect,' she continued lying, clearly knowing that Nick and his obnoxious face would get a good beating and he most likely would end up being raped.

'Life, huh?' he said and licked his lips. 'You cops have your way around the system. Arrange me a proper coffee in the morning. Coffee, like the ones steaming in front of you, not the brown piss they serve in here and I'll tell you everything you need to know. Oh, and a cell with a view.'

And just like that, with a hollow promise for decent coffee and a wish for fame, an excited Nick began to answer our questions.

'... I found her hiding in one of the lifeboats on the upper deck. She hid below the covers, snacks and everything with her. She begged me not to tell her teachers where she was. Cried out a soap opera story about her abusive mother,' Nick said and paused to take a sip out of his aromatic coffee. 'She even offered to pay me for my silence.'

'What happened next?' I asked, seeing that Nick was taking his time with devouring his coffee.

'I lied to her that the lifeboats were checked daily. She panicked and I told her not to worry. As she was going to pay me, I would take care of her. She and her lovely blonde hair. I sneaked her into an empty worker's cabin below. There, she became mine. My own. My number four,' he announced proudly.

'And the girl's body?' Ioli asked.

'Huh?' he said, coming out of his daydream of reliving the moment.

'The body,' Ioli said, trying to remain cool.

'Oh, I threw it overboard wrapped up in a plastic bag. There's a chute in the engine room. Opened it and out she went. I'm impressed she hasn't washed up somewhere by now. That's weird. I didn't use anything for extra weight. Refugees pop up on beaches all the time.'

Ioli stood up. 'You are one hell of a piece of shit. A total waste of oxygen. People like you is why we should still hang criminals. Have fun, inside. Hope you become someone's new bitch, to rape and to hold till death do you apart.'

She did not wait for a reply and stormed out the room.

'Was it something I said?'

'Shut it, Nick,' I said and stood up, pushing back my chair that reluctantly screeched upon the dirty tiles.

'See you in court, buddy,' he called out to me as the two guards lifted him up and I approached the door.

After thanking the prison warden and sorting out details of the recorded session with Nick, I headed outside.

Ioli stood by the car, enjoying the fresh air. The rain had ceased and faint sunrays skipped upon newborn puddles; the timid sun infusing the winter sky with shades of orange.

'Are we off duty, now, boss?' she asked.

'Err, yes.'

'Great. I haven't gotten wasted in a long time. Last decent drink was before my pregnancy,' she said and jumped in the car, placing her hands steady on the wheel.

'Food, first?'

'Of course,' she replied and stepped on the gas.

Greek meat, Greek ouzo. The Greek way of moving on.

Another day, another breath, another struggle, another case.

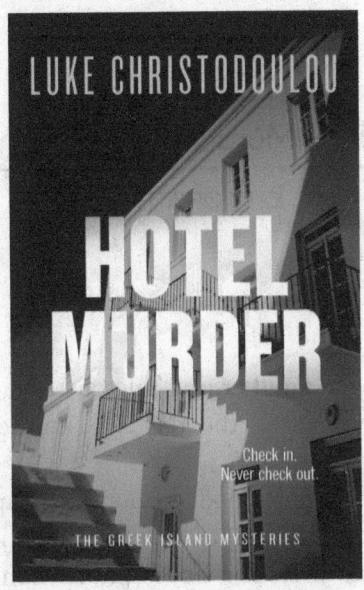

Hotel Murder: Chapter One

CITY OF ATHENS

It could have been another dull Tuesday. Yet, the day would go down in history as the day she murdered both her children.

Despoina Lemoni stood motionless, trapped between the dirty oven and the empty fridge; trapped in a life she no longer wished to live. The house phone hung by her side, slightly swinging by its faded-yellow twisted cord. She could not bear to hear another word. The menacing voices roaming around her mind's darkest corners were enough noise.

'What's wrong, Mummy?' her three-year-old daughter asked, lifting her head out of her Minnie Mouse coloring book. She sat, cold and hungry, leaning on the worn-in kitchen table, wondering why her mother was sad, day in, day out. A pale ghost of a being that was once her mother. Lina raised her voice and finally caught her mother's attention.

'Nothing,' Despoina mumbled in reply, scared of the

wild thoughts being born inside her head. She had not yet digested what her husband had just revealed to her.

Lina looked across the table at her infant sister. At least she always smiled at her. The nine-month-old baby happily banged her pink rattle upon the checkered blue-and-white vinyl tablecloth; both colors unable to hide the stains of ketchup, oil and other condiments that had fallen to its surface over the course of the last few months.

Five months had passed already since Despoina lost her house.

'Lost my house!' she grumbled. She hated that sentence. 'I did not *lose* my house. The bank took it away.'

Despoina gazed up and for a few serene moments looked out of her narrow basement window at the feet rushing to work on the cement pavement above; the dark clouds forming above only adding to their haste. Black shoes, brown shoes, flats, high heels, boots... all zoomed by her trembling watery eyes. She craved for a job to rush to. Her *old usual* Monday whining at work seemed ridiculous now. 'You never truly appreciate what you've got till it's gone,' her Nanna used to say. Now, Despoina realized how right she was.

Soon, fat drops dived out of the grey sky and fell to the deteriorating neighborhood below. Despoina had dragged herself to the front door, and for some reason stepped out into the rain. She used to hate getting caught in the rain. The cold water sank deep into her beige blouse, while her blood seethed beneath her icy skin. All around her were signs depicting prosperity long gone. Closed shops, rundown buildings, dead trees, and piles of trash.

'Fucking crisis,' she said, the words marinated in anger and sorrow. Her fingertips ran across her face, her nails cutting into her olive complexion. Bloody rivulets quickly blossomed. She stepped back into her home, slamming the squeaking, begging-for-a-paint door behind her.

In automated *mother-mode* she spent the rest of the evening cooking chicken nuggets and rice for her and Lina, bottle fed Antonia, bathed both girls, dressed them for sleep and put them to bed.

'Mummy?' Lina called out, watching her breath turn into a shadowy cloud, stopping her mother as she rushed to switch off her light. 'Can you tell me a fairy tale, Mummy?' she asked with hope.

'There's no such thing,' Despoina replied and left the room, mumbling how there would never be a happy ending.

Despoina raised her head high and wiped away her tears. She exhaled deeply, sure of what she had decided was needed to be done. She ambled into the kitchen and opened the top wooden cupboard, taking out a bottle of cheap red wine. Two years ago, she would not have even used it in cooking. But that was then, and this was now. No more wine-marinated octopus and fancy food for Despoina.

Both she and her husband heard the terrifying words that petrified every parent with a mortgage. 'We are going to have to let you go'.

Despoina fell back into her ripped armchair, pushing her dying-for-a-dye blonde hair over the top of its burgundy back. She brought the wine to her lips as she turned on the radio. Love songs and rain. She always loved the combination. With eyes forcibly shut, she daydreamed of moments lived, yet vanished into oblivion. Paradise lost. That's what the Greeks had, according to her.

Window-shaking thunder startled her. She had dozed off. An hour had passed since the last drop of fruity wine. Brought-up religiously, Despoina had no doubt about the eternity of the soul. Life on earth was a mere blip on the line of our existence.

'It's for their own good. I will not have them eating trash and being ridiculed about their father...' she whispered, lifting herself out of the rocking armchair.

With slow steps, she approached the kitchen sink and splashed frigid water upon her sallow face. She dawdled back to her children's door. Each step was harder to make. In her trembling right hand, she held her heavy pillow. Without another bedroom in the hole-of-a-house, she slept on the living room sofa.

Her hand froze upon the shiny door knob. Despoina closed her eyes and sighed as she quietly opened the door. The lone light came from a Disney princess night lamp. Placed on the floor between the bed and the cot, it cast a dim pink glow; just about enough light for Despoina to see her sleeping babies. She sat by Lina and gently caressed her hair; her mind splicing heavy knots in her alcohol-filled stomach.

'I love you, my beautiful,' she managed to utter, her throat clogging up. The pillow came down hard on Lina's small face. The young girl awoke, unable to breathe. Despoina kept both hands on the pillow and pushed down, while looking away. Soon, the girl's kicks ceased, and silence returned to the dark room.

Three hours to bring her into the world and three minutes to take her out of it.

Antonia was next, and in less time, she followed the fate of her lifeless sister.

The first rays sailed from the timid winter sun and reached the bedroom window, forcing the darkness to shrivel into shadows. The two dead girls lay in their beds. Eternal sleep, offered by the hands of the woman that brought them to life. Down the narrow hallway, another body sat against the chipped, riddled with mold wall.

Despoina had loaded her husband's hunting rifle, prayed to the Lord for forgiveness and brought the cold gun barrel to her quivering chin. She closed her eyes, and as her last tear journeyed down her cheek, Despoina found the courage to pull the trigger. A film-noir fan, she always joked about how she wanted to go out with a bang.

The police found her with her head blown open, yet with a smile permanently frozen on her. The wall behind her was sprayed with crimson blood and parts of her tormented brain. She hated that wall. Poetic revenge, she would have called it.

The neighbors gathered in shock and watched as the paramedics carried out the tiny lifeless body of Antonia, the body of the happy girl next door -Lina's golden locks were blowing in the wind out from beneath the white sheet-, and the bloody body of the woman who would haunt their everyday conversations. They were also struggling. The economic crisis had brought them all to their knees. Despoina's acts of death caused daily riots and fuelled the anger against the government's strict austerity program. Her murderous ways were analyzed by *experts* of every kind. Newspapers, news, blogs all featured the story.

But, like every tragedy in history, it became exactly that. History. People moved on to the next hot topic of the month, and new austerity measures kept being announced.

Hotel Murder: Chapter Two

Valentina stared at her phone's screen in amazement. Her alarm was set to go off in just nine minutes. *Great. Dear brain, thank you! Thank you for keeping me up all night thinking of things that I worry about all day.*

She rubbed her tired eyes as the illuminating light from her cell died out and pitch black governed the room once more. Sleepily, she kicked back the heavy mint-green quilt, hoping to fight off the drowsy heat invading from the wall radiator. Turning to her side, her hand brushed against Alexandro's bare back. She still could not get used to having a man in her house, in her life, in her heart. She hugged his naked body from behind and breathed in his 'man-smell'. She never could find the right title for it. He was her first; she had no other *naked sleeping man smell* to compare it to. She gently laid her lips upon his neck and reluctantly slid out of the king size bed. She tiptoed to the door, avoiding the parade of her shoes in front of the wooden wardrobe. She needed to take nothing. She had taken her make-up, clothes and shoes for the day, into the living room, the night before. Alexandro worked late, interrogating suspects in a case involving manslaughter at a nightclub while she was on duty with the crack of the Greek dawn. Being a parking enforcement officer was as boring as it sounds, yet Valentina did not mind the long shifts in all weather conditions, handing out tickets and arguing with vexed Athenian drivers. She was in the big city, away from her rock-of-an-island, and she had the whole package. An apartment, a job and a man.

Forty minutes later, a uniform-wearing Valentina walked out the front door; her platinum blonde hair rolled-up into a bun, her lips graced with bright red lipstick and her stomach filled with two pieces of bread, covered in Nutella, and a sizzling hot milky coffee.

She locked the stained chestnut fiberglass door and sighed. Before her eyes, once again hung a metallic six. Valentina turned the number upright again and pushed down with force. Apartment nine's only issue -the unscrewed number.

'Let's remind Alex, once again, to fix it,' she whispered the mental note, her mind laughing at the image of the mug she had bought him on a weekend escape. *When a man says he will fix it, he'll fix it. No need to remind him every six months*, was written in bold black letters across the large white cup.

———————

Not so far away, in the neighborhoods on the other side of the Parthenon, I was also creeping out of my apartment. Nothing worse than the fury of an awoken-before-her-time American, short-fused spouse.

I stood in front of the dirty hall mirror. The reflection staring back at me was finally one that caused me to smile. After a long two-year battle with cancer, I had started to regain weight -not too hard taking into account my undying love for street food and red meat; my color had returned to a healthy Greek white, and short, thin, brown hair had appeared back on my scalp, helping to shake off the unattractive image of my egg-shaped head. Most bald men look sexy; I looked like Humpty Dumpty's not-so-well-known Greek cousin.

Ioli Cara's phone call had abruptly popped my dream bubble -me standing between Messi and Ronaldo, celebrating with our fans, the top three soccer players in the world. Age fifty and still certain dreams remained the same. Though, back then, it was Maradona and Platini by my side.

'Sorry, boss, for waking you. I just got the fax from Interpol. The old guy had hidden property across Greece. All under fake names. Typical businessman avoiding taxes. There is a remote mansion in the meadows of Rhodes listed. Remember how his wife mentioned that he loved Rhodes as a child and that is why he built Anastos Tower by Rhode's port? I'm thinking if Scrooge is hiding out somewhere, this is the place. If he is not there, he is abroad. With money like his, he would need no passport.'

'You talk too much. How long have you been up?'

'An hour or so. Babies don't feed themselves, you know? Icarus has a Cretan appetite and an inner clock more precise than a Swiss watch,' she replied laughing.

'Okay, okay...' I had replied, jumping out of bed and rushing to the bathroom. Safe from Tracy's icy looks, I told Ioli to arrange the police ferry.

'Wait. Are we not sending local police? Is it worth us going out there on a hunch?'

'The fresh sea air will do us good. Besides, even if he is

there, we have no warrant. I'd rather it be just the two of us.'

'So that we can enter illegally, Captain Costa, Mr. Moral, Papacosta?'

'Well, if there was a suspicious sound coming from within...'

Ioli laughed again, and a light cry was heard from her infant son. 'Oh, no. The monster is moving. I'd better get out of here. Leave him to Mark. See you at headquarters,' she said hastily and the phone went silent.

Our case was not exactly *homicide-team material*, but three point seven billion to your name gets you attention. The chief placed half the task force on the case of the missing billionaire. Thanasis Zampetides, Greece's biggest shipping tycoon, aged seventy-two had vanished. His children reported him missing in a matter of hours. That was forty-three days ago. Most presumed the worst. The chief wanted no 'fuck-ups' as he so elegantly put it. He had the minister's office breathing down his neck, and he wanted to make sure that if the old guy's body turned up, his best officers were on the case.

Weeks of searching by police and private investigators, and unlimited airtime and press space offered zero results.

Ioli's gut instinct had always helped us solve cases in the past. Ioli felt certain that Mr. Zampetides, for reasons unknown, was taking time away from his hectic world of running Greece's largest shipping company. Having read through his biography, and after interviewing his wife, she was sure that the missing billionaire -as a free spirit, a child of the 60s- was somewhere *relaxing*. Taking time away from his daily life. The police had eliminated the possibility of kidnapping as the security cameras showed him leaving his

Athenian skyscraper alone and no ransom demands had ever been made.

To be completely honest, though intrigued by the mysterious lack of evidence, I did not deposit much of my time into the case. I had a pile of paperwork to attend to before my paper tower surpassed Pisa's as the world's tallest leaning tower, I had two court appearances to prepare for, and I preferred cases closer to home. The butchered homeless man behind Omonoia's square was far more deserving of my attention.

Ioli though needed to silence her gut. She began investigating places the billionaire could be. And with her known determination, fast forward forty-three days later, and we were set for the spear-shaped island of Rhodes.

Hotel Murder: Chapter Three

The crisp winter night succeeded the short rainy winter day and Valentina returned home, hungry, exhausted and soaking wet.

'What a shitty day,' she said as she kicked off her black shoes, offering much-needed relief to her swollen ankles. 'That's how honest money is made, Valentina,' she mimicked her father's deep bass voice. New to the force, she was the lowest ranking officer on the traffic department's totem pole. With the austerity measures holding back any hope for new recruits, she knew well that long shifts and busy streets would always be assigned to her. She also knew that in today's Greece having any sort of job was a blessing, so Valentina kept her whining to herself. Unemployment rate was closing in near to twenty percent. She could not comprehend how one in five was without a job. *These are surely terrifying times,*' she thought.

Closing the heavy door and leaving the outside world behind her, her eye caught a glimpse of a shiny magnolia envelope that lay on the scratched laminated flooring.

Bending down, she picked it up and flipped it around. Fancy, bold red letters covered its side.

HOTEL MURDER.

'The mystery weekend experience of a lifetime,' Valentina read the smaller subtitle. The next line though was the one that caught her attention. 'Congratulations! You have won a FREE stay. Please open.'

Valentina's red nails slid into the paper, ripping the envelope open.

'Congratulations,' the letter wished once more.

'You are holding one of the thirty random invitations to the grand opening of Hotel Murder. This is an ambitious project, looking to make its mark on Greece's tourist map. A remote hotel, with five-star amenities, upon a majestic Greek Isle. With multiple actors and a devilishly cunning mystery, it is destined to entertain you.

For our first weekend, we have decided to offer thirty lucky winners a FULLY FREE stay. No strings attached what-so-ever. No hidden charges. Free transfer from Piraeus port, free stay, all meals and drinks 100% free, and free participation in the mystery. All we want is your opinion. Your feedback on this exciting new project is valuable to us!

So what are you waiting for? Bring your PLUS-ONE (also FREE -yes, the boss has gone crazy!) to Piraeus port on Friday, 2nd of December, 16:00 sharp. Return to Piraeus, Sunday night.

Still a disbeliever? Too good to be true?

Call for inquiries: 01 3478 9812.'

Valentina read the letter twice. *'Too good to be true?'*

She placed the envelope on her prized possession, an antique coffee table, similar to the one her Nana had in the house she grew up in, back on her home island of Folegandros. She rubbed her shoulders and walked into her bedroom. A hot steamy bath was all she could focus on for the time being. She shed off her work clothes and slid into the shower. Water dangerously close to boiling point attacked her skin, providing warmth to her body. She spread coconut shower gel across her neck and chest, while sniffing the mesmerizing aroma.

Fifteen minutes later, she drifted into the kitchen, comfortable pyjamas covering her relaxed slender figure. Now all she needed was a good strong Greek coffee to complete her after-work nirvana. With the blinds up, Valentina curled up on her bright magenta sofa and, with her coffee entrapped between her warm fingers, she stared out at the rain. Soon, the first sips travelled down her, warming her from the inside. Unwound, her attention fell to the Hotel Murder invitation.

Alexandro would love it, she thought. *Men and their mystery stories!*

She must have heard over a dozen times, Alexandro's retelling of how he cracked the case at a murder/mystery dinner in England while visiting a cousin. He was only eighteen at the time. Now, a homicide officer, she could picture him diving in and analyzing everything. Personally, she thought the whole idea sounded corny, but then again, *the things women do for their men.* And with that thought, she guzzled her hot beverage and took her phone into her hands.

One beep, two beeps... 'Hello?' a fruity youthful voice came through the receiver.

'Er, yeah. I found an invitation under my door... Hotel Murder?' she asked.

'Congratulations! Welcome to an experience of a lifetime...'

'And the horrific acting begins,' Valentina could not resist

thinking and interrupted the eager-to-inform employee. 'Yes, yes. So, it's completely free?'

'One hundred percent, ma'am. Just bring your invitation and if your invitation specifies it, your plus-one. The ship will be expecting you at 16:00 sharp, Friday 2nd of December.'

'Yes, I've already read that part. What island is the hotel on?'

'That is part of the mystery,' the surely-under-twenty-five-year-old man said.

'You serious? We won't know where we are heading?' Valentina said, bringing her knees up to her chest, placing her cold feet under the couch pillows.

'Rules of the management. They want to avoid people intruding the weekends. The storyline begins the moment you set foot on board. It will be an amazing...'

'Yeah, yeah. I'm sure. Okay, count us in. What details do you need for the reservations?'

'None. Just bring your invitations. Your identities and back-stories will be provided by a member of staff. See you on the dock next Friday. We are dying to meet you. Pun intended!'

Oh, God. And the nightmare begins!'

Alexandro and his muddy boots came home an hour later. Valentina stopped him at the door with a passionate kiss and a warning about his footwear.

'Mmm, what smells so freaking good?' he said, his droopy Greek nose opening its narrow nostrils like a hound dog on a mission. 'My baby been cooking?' he inquired as his arms reeled her closer and his wide hands explored her rear.

'You wish. After the day I've had, you're lucky I got up to greet you,' she replied, the corners of her lips travelling upwards. 'I ordered pork chops from that tavern you talk about more than me...'

'Meat Castle?' he interrupted her, his voice climbing the decibel scale fuelled by excitement and an empty stomach.

'That's the one,' Valentina replied as she was raised up into the air. Alexandro lowered her gently and laid a forceful kiss on her slightly cracked-from-the-cold lips. Nothing that a few drops of virgin olive oil could not fix; Valentina remembered her mama's home remedy.

'Love truly does pass through the stomach,' she said and laughed as Alexandro rushed to the wooden IKEA table.

Valentina enjoyed their dinner time -her favorite time with Alexandro. A workaholic and a 'gymaholic', his appetite was greater than any man she had ever met. She watched him over their candle-lit meals as he relished all sorts of meats. Valentina was not very fond of the kitchen, while he was an able cook. The nights he did not 'create' - his verb for his cuisine masterpieces- Valentina prepared something simple along the lines of spaghetti or burgers, or ordered from an array of choices. Neither of them was a fussy eater. With delight, she would witness him calm down from his hectic day and smile as he retold his daily adventures; she would even laugh at his rather unamusing jokes.

Finally, plates were licked clean, and the last drop of Merlot journeyed down his throat. Valentina had been waiting for that moment. 'I've got another surprise for you,' she said, and an enigmatic smile came to life below her round glover-green eyes.

'What's that, babe?' he replied, relaxed with his voice tone carrying the vast satisfaction his body was experiencing.

'Next Friday... you and I... murder/mystery weekend on an island. What do you say to that, mighty detective?'

Alexandro tilted his head slightly to the right and studied his girlfriend with the same manner he *read* suspects down at the station.

'You for real?'

'Realler than your love for Olympiakos,' she replied, unable to control her high-pitched laughter. 'God, talk about murdering proper grammar.'

'That's, err, great,' he said and got up to take his vacant plate to the sink.

'Why so unenthusiastic?' Valentina inquired, picking up the hesitant color in his words.

'No, no, Don't get me wrong. I just... well, not to sound like a party pooper, but can we afford this? I mean, Christmas is just around the corner, and I paid for all that shit to be fixed on my car last month...'

'Ssshh,' Valentina said, walking over to him and placing her index finger on his moving lips. 'You worry too much. Stress will be the death of you. I know our financial capabilities well. I won this weekend. It is completely free.'

His face lit up and his eyes opened wide. 'Seriously?'

'Yep, all-inclusive. Will not cost us a dime.'

Valentina swore that all the neighbors heard his cowboy yell of celebration and the loud kisses he placed on her lips and neck.

An hour later, Alexandro exited the shower, dried off and remained naked as he climbed into bed next to her. Valentina kept her eyes glued to her romance book, yet could not concentrate on the words blurring up before her. She knew well what was coming. Pork chops *and* a free getaway weekend? Alexandro was on top of the world. His hands teased her by invading under her bedtime T-shirt. She turned to look at him. She loved that goofy expression; his mischievous grin upon his flushed face. He knew all her buttons. In seconds, Nora Roberts fell to the floor, followed by her underwear and purple T-shirt. His tongue, travelling from her belly upwards, sent shivers down her spine and shook her inner core. Though her only lover, Valentina believed they had great chemistry. When in her, she felt sexier than any romance heroine. Later, after a satisfying round of love making, she drifted off to sleep in his broad arms, beaming and content. Soon, both departed for dream land and visions of a spectacular and bewildering mystery weekend came to life in their mind's inner cinema.

Grab your copy…
vinci-books.com/HotelMurder

About the Author

Luke Christodoulou is an Amazon bestselling author, a poet and an English teacher (MA Applied Linguistics - University of Birmingham). He is, also, a coffee-movie-book-Nutella lover.

His first book, THE OLYMPUS KILLER (#1 Bestseller - Thrillers), was released in April, 2014. The book was voted Book Of The Month for May on Goodreads (Psychological Thrillers). The book continued to be a fan favorite on Goodreads and was voted BOTM for June in the group Nothing Better Than Reading. In October, it was BOTM in the group Ebook Miner, proving it was one of the most talked-about thrillers of 2014.

The second stand-alone thriller from the series, THE CHURCH MURDERS, was released April, 2015 to widespread critical and fan acclaim. The Church Murders became a bestseller in its categories throughout the summer and was nominated as Book Of The Month in three different Goodreads groups.

DEATH OF A BRIDE was the third Greek Island Mystery to be released. Released in April, 2016 it followed in the footsteps of its successful predecessors. From its first week in release it hit the number one spot for books set in Greece.

MURDER ON DISPLAY came out in 2017 and enriched the series.

HOTEL MURDER, the fifth and 'final' book in the series, followed in early 2018.

In 2018, his box set of mysteries became an international bestseller.

Luke Christodoulou has also ventured into 'children's book land' and released 24 MODERNIZED AESOP FABLES, retelling old stories with new elements and settings. The book, also, features sections for parents, which include discussions, questions, games and activities.

In 2019, TWELVE MONTHS OF MURDER came out, his first collection of shorts.

His first novel outside of the Greek Island Mysteries collection came in 2020, maintaining his love for a Greek theme. A supernatural thrill ride with the name of BEWARE OF GREEKS BEARING GIFTS.

PANDORA'S BOX followed in 2021. A mind-twisting whodunit set in his favorite Greek town, the seaside resort of Parga. The following year saw the release of the highly anticipated ACHILLES' HEEL.

His first YA murder mystery, SENIOR YEAR MURDERS was released in 2024, hitting the charts for young adult thrillers.

He is currently working on various projects (which he is secretive about).

He resides in Limassol, Cyprus with his loving wife, his chatty daughter and his super-energetic son.

Hobbies include travelling the Greek Islands discovering new food and possible murder sites for his stories. He, also, enjoys telling people that he 'kills people for a living'.

www.ingramcontent.com/pod-product-compliance
Lightning Source LLC
Chambersburg PA
CBHW011348010726
47493CB00011B/3000